FIRST PERSON,
THIRD SEX

FIRST PERSON, THIRD SEX

SLOANE BRITAIN

CUTTING EDGE

ISBN-13: 978-1-957868-85-1

Published by
Cutting Edge Books
PO Box 8212
Calabasas, CA 91372
www.cuttingedgebooks.com

CHAPTER ONE

M y reflection in the mirror smiled back at me. Not bad-looking, not bad-looking at all. Short fluffy blonde hair, light complexion with no blemishes, blue eyes, long black eyelashes, full lips and a nice straight nose. Might as well complete the picture, I'm five feet seven inches tall, weigh one hundred twenty pounds and wear a 34C. I don't know exactly what the rest of my measurements are but, take my word for it, they're more than just allright.

Yeah, I looked good. Twenty-one years old and I looked about nineteen and didn't feel a day over eighty. I liked looking at myself in the mirror that way sometimes. It made me feel good to remind myself that I had looks. Sometimes I did the mirror bit in order to remind myself that I didn't look any older than I was. Not only did I look young but my face had a soft gentle expression like a virgin's. That's one for the books!

I had just become legal a few months before but I always say that it's not the years but the mileage that counts. My face was like a speedometer that's been turned back. The old engine knew that it was time for a trade-in for a newer model. It wasn't likely that I'd be able to do that so I was settling for the next best thing, a complete overhaul.

That's why I was standing there in the bedroom making faces at myself in the mirror. I was taking a last look at myself before starting the remodeling job. I had just a few minutes left in which to be alone before my roommate would arrive. She was part of the rejuvenation campaign and so was the apartment. Outside of the summers when I had worked as a camp counselor I had always lived at home with my mother and father. The apartment was going to be my first experience in making a home of my own. I figured that would help me straighten myself out and the girl I was going to share the place with was just the sort of person I needed to have around because she was sweet and kind and didn't know much about me. I'll tell you more about her later. The most important part of my campaign was my new job. I was going to start teaching elementary school that fall. Being a teacher was so far removed from some of the things I had been doing that it was laughable. I didn't want to go on in the old way though and I was determined to go into teaching like I was taking on a new skin.

I guess it's time I introduced myself. My name is Paula Harman. I was born in Barrington, Connecticut, May 5th, 1938, attended the local public schools and graduated magna cum nothing from the nearby state teachers college. You already know what I look like and a little bit about what I felt like. Why? What made Paula Harman run? That's a long story, kiddies. I had time to think about some of it while I was waiting for my roommate to arrive. I was remembering my life the way people will take a long look at a house they're leaving and never expect to see again. Good or bad, happy or unhappy a house where you've lived or a phase of your life that's over is something you want to fix in your memory.

My mother's name is Grace. On my birth certificate it says that my father's name is George Harman and the guy who shares my mother's bedroom has the same name. As far as I'm concerned that's as far as it goes. The way I feel about it, I didn't have a real father except in the legal and biological meaning of the word. That's why I stopped calling him Dad when I was ten years old. It used to burn him up when I called him George or just plain Harman. I didn't like making him mad that way, I wasn't out to fight with him or hurt him or anything like that, what I really wanted was for him to just quietly disappear. I couldn't call him father or dad or pop or anything like that because every time I even thought about him that way it made me want to cry.

By the time I got to high school there was no more problem about that because he wasn't around for me to talk to. He wasn't dead and he hadn't divorced my mother but a hell of a lot of difference that made. He might as well have been dead for all the good he was to Mom and me. He lived in the same house with us and even ate a few meals there. Most of the time he didn't make it home for dinner. More often he came rolling in in the early hours of the morning and flopped right into bed to sleep snoring drunkenly. There were plenty of nights when he didn't show up at all. Two or three days would go by before he would be back nursing a mammoth hangover.

He always got up in the morning just in time to rush cursing out of the house to work. My father's drinking never kept him from missing a day's work nor was he ever late because of morning after blues. He wasn't an alcoholic. He wouldn't dream of drinking alone and only sopped it up when he was out making it with a chick half his age—and that was most of the time.

George Harmon didn't let his social life interfere with his job. He had worked himself up the hard way to being purchasing agent for a typewriter factory and he was too proud of his success to jeopardize it. The women (girls really) were strictly for after work and weekends—almost any night and almost any woman if she was free, white (or any other color short of purple) and under twenty-one. I don't know when I first learned about my father nor exactly how. How do you learn the Star Spangled Banner? Some things a kid learns automatically because she lives in a place where everybody has knowledge of them. She absorbs them through something like osmosis. Everybody in Barrington knew about my father like they knew who was President and I got the scoop on my old man before I learned to take my thumb out of my mouth and place it against the tip of my nose.

Even though he made good money at his job we didn't see much of it. He paid the rent and utility bills regularly. Everything else was a question of luck. Some weeks he would turn his entire salary over to Mom. Then a month or more might go by where her requests for money would be met with cruses and threats of physical violence. It didn't do her any good to go through his pockets when he was asleep at those times. She always found that what he had told her was true. There would be only a dollar or two left in his wallet from his salary. Young girls like to be given nice presents—it keeps them happy—and willing.

Mom had to work in a dress shop to support herself and me. As soon as I was old enough to go to work I got a job after school waiting on tables in a diner. I didn't make enough to support us so Mom had to continue working. Besides, she would only take ten dollars a week from me for my room and board. She wanted me to save the money I earned so that I'd be able to go to college.

I never could understand why my mother put up with it. She stood on her feet for eight hours every day in the dress shop and that's no joke when you get past forty. She worked in the swanki-est women's store in town selling dresses that she could never afford to buy for herself. Lots of times she sold expensive dresses to the girls who came in there shopping with the money her own husband had given them.

I just didn't get it. Why didn't she just kick the no good bastard out? Heaven knows what she needed him for. We could have gotten along without the few bucks he tossed our way like throwing bones to a dog. And she knew he was unfaithful to her. Hell! the whole town knew it. It was a local joke the way George Harman threw his money away on teen-age whores. He was something of an institution. Every town has its village idiot and maybe every other town besides Barrington has its sucker for a young piece too. The humiliation of being his daughter damn near killed me and it must have been hell to be patroniz-ingly pitied by everybody as Mom was. Once I asked her why she wouldn't tell him to go to hell and clear out after the rotten way he had been treating her for so many years.

"Leave George?" she replied incredulously. "Why, I couldn't do that. I know he's got his faults but I believe that all that will change. It's just a phase he's going through. Young men have to sow their wild oats. He'll settle down in a few more years and we'll just forget about the past then and live together like any other family. Besides, even if he never changes, I couldn't leave George. I couldn't live without him. You see, Paula, I love your father as much now as I did when I first married him. You're young and you can't understand these things but some day you'll know what it means to love a man so much you'll put up with anything just to keep him."

Her pretty little speech made me want to puke. I felt as though my mother was a hopeless case. I mean, what can you expect from a cretin even if she is your own mother? Hearing her talk that way didn't make me feel so good about myself either. Some chance I'd have with a heredity like that: the daughter of a woman with her brains in a sack and a father with his brains all in his trousers.

My mother's idiotic mouthings about her no good husband set my mind straight on one thing. Never, I vowed to myself, never will I let any man use and abuse me the way she does. It wasn't going to be any moronic character out of a torch song. That "it doesn't matter what my man does I am his for evermore" bit wasn't for me. I was going to put the shoe on the other foot and I started in real young to do it.

I was fifteen and a junior in high school when I got the job in the diner by lying about my age. I could pass for eighteen then because my body was already fully developed and the sort of home life I had had showed in the guarded expression on my face which was more like an adult's. When I was looking in the mirror and thinking about all this I was twenty-one and looked nineteen. Funny how you can get younger as you get older. I believe that the day I got my college diploma (which I had never really believed I'd get until the day I did) the clock was turned back three years for me. Knowing that I was capable of accomplishing something I had set out to do made me feel younger. It restored a bit of youthful optimism to me.

Anyway, I worked in the diner from five p.m. until nine-thirty Monday through Saturday. It wasn't too bad. There would be a big rush around dinner time and I'd be kept hopping but the place usually quieted down by seven-thirty and from then on all I'd have to do was serve pie and coffee to the truck drivers and motorists who came in. The only trouble was that in those days there weren't many part-time jobs available for minors in Barrington and I had to settle for what I could get. Salary-wise it wasn't much. The tips were small too because the only people who ate in the diner were the ones who couldn't afford to go anywhere else. It was a bad time in Barrington because a lot of the people who had moved there during the war to work in the factories had stayed on and there wasn't enough work to go around.

I was lucky that I found any job at all. Truth was I made enough to cover expenses and still have a chunk left to put away towards college. Trouble was that I got like an animal that's tasted blood, the experience of making money and having a few nickels to squander recklessly in mad hedonistic splurges went to my head. I started wanting to have more and more. My taste was in my feet in those days. I thought all the garish junk I saw in the jewelry store windows was beautiful just because I couldn't afford it. It used to really stick in my craw when I'd see some real classy thing that I wanted but couldn't buy. I had to lay my hands on more loot and it didn't take me long to figure out how. I just had to follow the family tradition. The sins of the father taught the child a lesson. Wonder how it would look embroidered on a sampler? ... "Do unto others before they do unto you."

My boss was a fat old Greek guy with a yellow complexion and teeth to match. When he opened his mouth he looked real weird because his teeth being the same color as his face made it look as if he had skin growing inside his mouth. He used to stand behind the cash register in the diner staring at me as if I were a prime cut of beef. I was real flattered, it was like being eyed by a dyspeptic walrus. At first I ignored him but when the itch for the root of all something or other got real bad I reconsidered. What the hell, the old bastard had plenty of loot and if I didn't take it from him some other woman would.

It wasn't long before I had him so weak for me it was pathetic. I held out for getting my terms, meanwhile swinging my hips around the diner for all I was worth. The gook nearly went crazy. He knew what I was holding out for but he resisted giving it to me as long as he could bear not getting his goodies. Not that he hadn't been nuts for the chance to get at me as soon as he saw me. Hell no, right from the start he would have given anything to get his sweaty mitts on my body. For the pleasure of feeling my fresh young skin naked beneath his sour smelling body he would have given an arm, a leg, a year off his life, anything except money. The old man made a small fortune off his diner but it killed him to spend a nickel of it. I had to work on him for a month before he changed his mind. I put on a real good performance, if I do say so myself. He never got a straight look from me, it was all sidelong glances with the fluttering eyelashes bit. I used to get up real close to him and then bend over to pick up something so that he could sneak a peek down the front of my uniform. He came around to my way of thinking.

The first time he was overly excited from waiting so long so it was no good. It was over in less than a minute. That didn't make any difference to me, I wanted all the cash we had agreed upon. I wanted thirty bucks from him each time we were together even if all he wanted was to hold my hand. He paid me a salary for working for him in the diner and everything else was extra. What difference did it make what we did when we were together? Whether he wanted sex or not I was spending my valuable time with him and he'd have to pay the price. The boss cursed and threatened me but I held firm until the three tens were in my hand.

He paid every time after that too. It killed him to part with the greenbacks. Each time he got so depressed that it took him a week to get over it. By the end of the week he was hot for me again and willing to shell out for what he wanted. All he wanted for his money was my body, he didn't seem to expect me to react nor did he care whether or not I even bothered to put on an act as if I were enjoying myself.

It was different with the short order cook. With him I really had to put on a show. He said he didn't enjoy it unless the girl was getting her kicks too. I started making it with him shortly after I had learned from our boss how easy it was. All I had to do was keep each of them from catching on that I was balling the other and I had it made.

Rauol, the cook, could only afford ten dollars but I figured every little bit helps. Besides, he wasn't so hard to take. He was a goodlooking young Puerto Rican boy who spoke little English and communicated with me mostly through facial expressions and gestures. He was a sweet goodnatured guy who was a little lost outside of his native country. I really liked him as a person and that made going to bed with him easier. It was even pleasant to pretend that I was enjoying it because of the way Rauol's face lit up when I sighed and moaned in pretended pleasure. He was gentle with me, taking his time, caressing the tips of my breasts, kissing me all over my body, using his hands expertly to arouse me before he entered. It didn't do any good though. I could feel his body moving against mine but the sensation never became anything more than one of touch.

No matter what either of the men did to me I felt no pleasure … nothing … it was like I was dead inside. I just played my part like an actress giving a performance and waited until the man finished. The sooner the better because, while not terribly disagreeable, the whole thing struck me as faintly ridiculous and I had to force myself to keep from laughing out loud.

I had an easy excuse made up for myself. I told myself that I wasn't responding because I was motivated by greed and not by love. I felt like laughing because, well, let's admit it, if you're not feeling anything there is something absolutely absurd about normally self-contained dignified human beings grunting and panting with that expression of complete absorption on their faces. The positions are really something too. Try it sometime, think about the weird contortions people get into when they're having sex; only picture them in those positions when they're doing something else like reading a book or playing Monopoly. Face it, the image is uproariously funny.

I had it all figured out that I would feel the same ecstacy that other people did if I were with a man I loved and that there was nothing unusual about me. In brief, I tried to convince myself that frigidity was negotiable. Of course I never put my theories to the test by having a real love affair with a man. Honest, Rauol and my boss were the only men whom I ever let come near me. I didn't even date much and when I did go out with a guy I made sure that I got home at the end of the evening without any hanky-panky along the way. There were a variety of reasons for the Miss Prim act. The one I stuck to the most was a fear of having anyone in that town think that I was an immoral slob like my father. My little friends from the diner didn't count because they wouldn't dare let anyone know about our relationship. Don't forget, I was jail bait. It was the boys around my own age that I was leary of. I wasn't going to have those walking pimples sniggering about me in the locker room. It wasn't until the summer of the year when I graduated from college that I found out that there was another reason, a reason that accounted for a lot of things.

Back to the ranch. I swung along with my two culinary lotharios for quite a while having a ball buying myself all sorts of junk that I didn't need with the money they gave me. Guess I got too cocky, I had been getting away with so much murder that it was hard to believe it would ever end. I paid less and less attention to keeping my secret until one night when I was so careless I might as well have put a signboard on my back. I'll skip the gory details for now. Briefly, the boss caught Rauol and me in a situation that left no room for interpretation. It was quite a scene.

Because I was young and could run fast I managed to escape with my life. I walked into the house looking like something the cat had dragged in then changed its mind about and dragged out again. Mom nearly fainted when she saw me. Luckily, she's so gone in that little world she's created for herself that she believed the phony story I told her.

I was thinking about that night when everything suddenly blew up in my face when I heard my roommate and her parents coming up the stairs. Janet came into the apartment, her arms loaded with clothes, books and lots of mysterious looking little brown bags.

"Hi," Janet gasped, "I'll have the rest of this stuff up here in about eighty or ninety more trips and then we can send my parents on their way and have a nice long talk. Boy, have I got a lot to tell you. What a summer this has been!"

Janet's mother, Mrs. Coxe, came into the room at that moment and stage whispered conspiratorially to me, "Oh, I'm sure it's been quite a summer. Her father and I got letters all summer long that began with 'I am fine how are you and ended with 'Well, I haven't really much to say'—with a request for cookies and some new tennis balls sandwiched in between. Must have been quite a summer indeed! The only time I ever wrote that kind of letter to my family was when I met Janet's father. They put up with that kind of drivel for three months until I finally phoned them from Niagara Falls. They had known what was going on all the time and I had thought I was being so smart."

Mrs. Coxe laughed richly and looked at her daughter with warm affection in which there was but the smallest amount of anxiety mixed in.

"That's right, Ma," Janet responded. "His name's Alphonse and he's a taper-snuffer by trade. Things have been pretty slow lately but Alphonse doesn't lose heart. He knows that electric lights are only a passing fad and soon there'll be a demand for a man with his talents. And I'm just wild about the way he twirls his long black moustache when he looks at me."

Mrs. Coxe laughed, a little too heartily I thought, and went to the door where her husband was struggling. Janet had stuffed enough luggage for a trip around the world into their little car. I pitched in and between the four of us we managed to get the car unloaded in about twenty minutes.

After her parents had left, a strange mood seemed to settle over Janet. Instead of having that long girly-girly talk she had spoken of before, Janet moved around the apartment with her eyes downcast, desultorily picking up things and putting them down again in inappropriate places. I was busy unpacking but I couldn't help noticing that there was terrific tension in the air. I got kind of panicky wondering if I had made a mistake. Was Janet Coxe really the sort of girl I had thought she was? Could we really be friends? We were almost strangers to each other and yet we were going to live together.

We had known each other all through college but neither of us had taken much notice of the other until shortly before graduation. The Oakwood Elementary School notified both of us on the same day that we were hired for teaching jobs that fall.

A celebration was held in the student lounge. There was a melancholy about such gatherings which each of us tried to hide from the others. We were all preoccupied with what was before us. Soon we would have to face the responsibilities and loneliness of being teachers, living in unfamiliar surroundings, being accountable to school administrators, the P. T.A., the standards of adult society and, most demanding of all, our own matured consciences. We laughed and joked and wished each other luck, savouring the swiftly fleeting moments of youthful comradery.

After the others left, Janet and I stayed on in the student lounge talking As though our notices of appointment were certificates of adulthood, we dropped the facade of adolescent eagerness and told each other of our doubts and fears. Neither of us had ever spoken so openly to anyone before. We got to know more about each other that afternoon than we had learned during all the four years of our acquaintance.

I began to really dig that girl. Listening to Janet talking about loneliness and feelings of inadequacy, I realized that someone else had problems like mine. We couldn't have been more different on the surface and our lives had little in common but the things that really count are the deep inner emotions and we were like two peas in the same unselfconfident pod there. We had just acted out the same emotions in different ways.

Janet was the last person I had ever expected to have doubts about herself. I've already told you that I think I'm goodlooking but that's only something I know intellectually. In spite of all evidence to the contrary, down deep inside myself I didn't really believe that I was as pretty as most of the other girls in my class. It knocked me out to learn that Janet felt the same way about herself. She's very attractive with green eyes, a milk-white complexion, long black hair and a soft sexy figure.

I had always taken it for granted that she was just an ordinary happy-go-lucky college kid, only a lot more beautiful than most. Listening to her talk that afternoon I became aware of a difference in the girl … an unsureness which reached out to me and reminded me of how often I had wished for a friend who would know without my having to tell her of the many empty hurting places.

We discussed the Oakwood Elementary School and the new jobs we would be assuming in the fall. It was exciting and challenging to think about finally being on the other side of the classroom desk but moving to a new city would mean other things as well. There were practical problems to be confronted. Janet confessed to feeling overwhelmed by the sudden realization that she would soon be responsible for finding and maintaining her own home, doing her own cooking, arranging her transportation. As the youngest of a family of six which had lived in the same town for forty years she had never had to consider these things before. Her parents had always taken care of practical matters so that Janet would have her mind free for her studies. Now she would have to grow up in a hurry. The baby bird was leaving the nest, it was time for her to learn to fly—Janet said she would be satisfied if she managed a crawl.

I was worried about the same things. I knew more about life than Janet did but it wasn't the kind of knowledge which would help me get along in Oakwood. I wouldn't be giving courses in my specialty at the Oakwood Elementary School. Too bad, it was the one subject in which I considered myself to be an expert. At twenty-one I had already earned a Ph.D. from the school of hard knocks.

I had learned a lot and learned it fast. I was much better equipped to face adult life than Janet was. It occurred to me that if we shared an apartment I could help the poor kid make the transition from living at home to being on her own. Also, as we talked, I was aware of a selfish desire to keep Janet close to me. I wanted to spend a lot of time with this green-eyed beauty. It would be marvelous if we could spend many more hours in this kind of intimate conversation. I wanted to be able to look at Janet's gorgeous face until I had my fill. I had never before realized quite how beautiful Janet really was. Now she seemed so lovely that I longed to live with her as I would long for possession of a beautiful painting which I could keep in my home and enjoy its perfection as much as I liked. Also, I felt a tenderness toward her that was like nothing I had ever felt toward another human being. I wanted to protect her, keep the fragile flower of her innocence from harm. I yearned to gather Janet in my arms and hold her close, blocking out the rest of the world and all the things that had hurt her in the past and could hurt her in the future.

As we continued to talk, my determination to have Janet live with me grew. I didn't understand why I was feeling so much emotion towards this girl and I didn't bother analyzing my feelings at the time. The important thing was to make sure that we would be roommates in the fall. I could figure out the crazy longing to gather Janet in my arms and clasp her to my breast in an embrace of protective tenderness—and something else that I couldn't admit even to myself at the time—when I was alone and had time to think.

I suggested that we get an apartment together. To my vast pleasure, Janet agreed instantly. She said it would be great if we could live together. That way we could get to know everything about each other. She wanted to get to know everything about me. The afternoon's sample had convinced her that deeper knowledge of me would reveal many similarities between us.

I couldn't have put it better. Janet seemed to be the first person I had ever met who might feel about music and books and painting as I did. In spite of the outwardly wanton pattern of my life these were the things that really mattered to me. More important, Janet might even see life as I did ... as a tragedy so overwhelmingly miserable that it became almost ridiculous and comic through the intensity of its horrors which were like absurd exaggerations that became parodies of themselves. Yes, I wanted very much to live with Janet and perhaps (oh hope too strong to ever be satisfied) lose with her the constant feeling of aloneness that never left me even when I was with groups of people.

Janet's uncle, who had a real estate office in a town near Oakwood, located an apartment for us. It was a three room furnished flat built above a former stable that had been converted into a garage. It was within walking distance of the school and cheap enough so that we would be able to pay the monthly rent and still save some money toward traveling during our summer vacations. After all, we were going to be school teachers and didn't all school teachers take trips somewhere, anywhere, during their vacations?

We parted for the summer. Janet was going to work as a waterfront instructor at a resort and I had my usual summer's job as a camp counselor. During the two months we were parted for the summer we exchanged occasional postcards and a couple of phone calls to confirm plans for the fall.

Then September had rushed in upon us and we both had been forced to realize that we were going off to a strange town, to do unfamiliar work and to live with someone known to us only as a "good Joe."

Janet interrupted my reflections. "Having given the matter considerable thought," she said, coming out of the bedroom and into the living room where I had been sitting, "I have come to the conclusion that it will take me until next April to get all my things put away. So, I have decided not to knock myself out right away and instead invite you to join me in a coffee break."

"Sure," I said and smiled.

And Janet smiled back at me and as our eyes met in a look of mutual affection I knew that everything was going to be alright, that sharing this apartment was the best idea either of us had ever had.

I asked Janet what all the marvellous things that had happened to her that summer were. She had seemed so anxious to talk about it before.

"It's funny, Paula, until I saw you here in the apartment, I felt differently. I thought I had had the most exciting summer of my life. Now it all seems silly. The really important things are all here in Oakwood with you and the school."

My heart lurched within me. I had to struggle to keep my voice from quavering as I said, "Well, tell me about it anyway."

"It's the usual story," Janet said. "I met a guy and we had a summer romance. When we were together at the resort he seemed wonderful. You know how those things are, some guy looks good when he's all tanned and running around with his muscles bulging all over the place and because it's summer and everybody is in a romantic mood you start thinking he's the perfect male. Now that I'm away from him, I couldn't care less. I don't want to ever see him again."

We continued talking for about an hour. I told Janet about my summer, the parts of it that it was right to tell her about. Then she went back to her unpacking and I settled down in the living room to write some letters.

Several hours later Janet came out again. She had just about finished with her unpacking and wanted to take another coffee break. She came upon me so quietly that I didn't hear her enter the room and went on with the letter I had been writing until she made me aware of her presence by speaking.

"Don't tell me you're homesick already?"

"Oh, no. I'm not writing home. I just wanted to tell a friend of mine all about our lovely new apartment."

I knew that Janet could tell from the expression in my eyes that I was lying. That I had been writing a letter of pleading and that whatever it was that I had been asking for from my friend, I didn't think Janet could give it to me.

We sat in our tiny living room, balancing the coffee cups on the arms of our chairs, talking about what we were going to do to the apartment to fix it up. It was furnished, obviously, with things that the landlord's wife had thrown out in fits of redecorating. The odds and ends of furnishings had less relation to period than they had in serviceability. The middle cushion of the couch sagged ominously as if it had played host to jumping children for so many years that now it had decided to go into retirement and was announcing the fact to the world. The chair in which I was sitting was a bad example of 1940 modern. The smooth flowing lines that looked so invitingly womb-like would have been comfortable for a foetus but I came to terms with it only by draping one leg over an arm of the chair and letting the other hang limply down from the edge of the seat.

Janet was talking loosely of white-washed walls, purple drapes and Kandinsky prints. Her long black hair looked soft and inviting in the lamplight. Her strong young face was deceptive now that I saw it at rest while Janet was concentrating more on her outlandish ideas than on the impression she was making. There was a vulnerability about Janet's face that disturbed me. What could ever have happened to that fresh white skin, that healthy athletic body, those fantastically long yet infinitely female legs, to make that hurt look play around the corners of Janet's eyes and hint of its presence in the lost way she smiled at me, constantly asking for my approval?

Knowing that tomorrow would of necessity be even more hectic than today as we would have to go down to the school and get our classrooms in order for the school opening in two days, we couldn't seem to stop talking nonsense to each other about redecorating. Like children trying to talk away the presence of the night, we laughed and gossiped until three that morning. At last weariness overcame us both. Reluctantly, we decided to go to bed.

Janet had been somewhat disappointed to find that we would have to take a three-room apartment instead of a four as she didn't care for the idea of sharing the bedroom. She had always had her own room at home and was not anxious to break with a pattern which had given her her only opportunity to be alone in a house that seemed to be always teeming with people.

She asked me which of the twin beds I would prefer. I hesitated only a moment before insisting that I would rather sleep on the studio couch in the living room. Regretting her selfish desire to have the room to herself and fearing that she had somehow communicated her thoughts to me, Janet assured me of how much she had been looking forward to lying in bed together in the dark and talking from bed to bed.

I listened to Janet and stared at her for a long hard minute before saying, "No." and gathering up the bedclothes, went into the living room.

An uneasy good-night shouted from room to room and sleep settled down like a mockingly temporary peace.

That is, Janet slept. I lay awake for hours thinking about my reasons for wanting to sleep in the living room. It was lousy of me to pull something like that without any explanation but there was nothing I could say. The last thing I wanted in the world was to hurt Janet. Yet, it was unthinkable that I explain my action by telling her of the tremendous change that had taken place in me during the summer. Janet mustn't know of the wildly beautiful, wonderfully lonely discovery I had made.

With a mixture of equal parts of happiness and sadness, I lay awake remembering the past months.

CHAPTER TWO

There was plenty wrong with my counseling job at Camp Mohawk but I loved it. I could do without the spoiled snotty-nosed kids who were my charges and the other counselors nearly drove me mad with their incessant talk about boy friends.

The older girls helped each other get away at night without being found out by the Camp directors. Directly across the lake from Camp Mohawk was a boys' camp, Camp Arrow. Within a week after the Camps opened for the summer the counselors from the two camps were paired off. There was a small heavily wooded island in the middle of the lake. The girls were supposed to stay in the camp every night taking care of the campers. They had one day a week off and were required back on Camp grounds by ten that evening. Only on the weekly joint picnic or dance or hike were the counselors from the two camps supposed to meet. That rule was about as effective as an ice-cube in a furnace. The counselors alternated in covering for each other. Under cover of night the girls quietly slid canoes into the water and paddled out to the island. The male counselors from Camp Arrow used a similar procedure. The couples would meet under the thick trees of the island and seek out densely wooded spots where they could be alone. Just before dawn the girls would paddle back to Camp. There were many wisecracks made about the white men shooting the Arrow into the Mohawk for a change.

That scene was definitely not for me. The other counselors nauseated me with their ceaseless talk about the adolescent creeps they spent the nights with on the island. They described everything that had transpired the night before, sparing no details. Black and blue marks on arms and shoulders were displayed proudly. Necks disfigured with teeth marks were flaunted like badges of honor.

I wanted to scream at them. Didn't they know that the little game they were playing could become deadly serious? What if there was a slip? What if one of the girls should get herself knocked up when she thought she was just playing a harmless game? They didn't play Scrabble out on that island at night! The counselors from Camp Arrow might be pimplyfaced adolescents just learning to shave but they were men and could give a girl something she hadn't bargained on. And whether it stretches, folds, bends, collapses, flows from a tube, squirts through a plastic nozzle or does handstands in Times Square, nothing is absolutely one hundred per cent safe. I was horrified to hear that most of the girls relied on the calendar to use a rhythm system. Didn't the idiots realize that that was about as reliable a forecaster as the weather report?

I tried to talk to them but they wouldn't listen so I gave up. They just refused to realize what it could mean to become pregnant and have to marry someone they'd hardly recognize in the daylight. I felt that I knew. For years I had had a nagging suspicion that my parents had to get married. That would explain the wedding when my mother was only seventeen and the grudging attitude of my father. I was almost sure that I had been conceived out of wedlock but something held me back from making sure by checking up on the date of my parent's marriage. Why didn't I just consult the county records and find out and stop all that silly speculation? Why does a child lie in bed at night thinking that the bogey man is in his room yet not turn the light on to find out? Sometimes there's greater safety in imagined fears, reality might hold worse ones. Besides, I already felt lousy enough about myself without finding out that I was a bastard too.

The camp director and assistant director were an elderly New England couple who lived in a cabin far from the rest of the camp and only emerged to spy on their personnel and check every figure in the accountant's books. The old couple would appear unexpectedly at a cabin, make a hurried yet minute inspection and disappear again in a matter of minutes after exhorting the counselor, "Fresh air and exercise, that's the ticket. You make sure the children get lots of sunshine and take part in all the sports activities. Yes sir, keep them healthy and happy." What a pair of birds those two were! Strictly from nowhere.

I didn't like the children, was bored by my fellow counsellors, was contemptuous of my bosses, wouldn't have anything to do with the boys from Camp Arrow and yet loved the job. Every year I looked forward all fall and winter to returning to Camp Mohawk. What I prized was the opportunity it afforded me to get out in the country, to swim and canoe and breath the fresh pine-scented air. It was like taking a vacation and getting paid for it.

There were other compensations too. The loot I took away from that place each summer made my enjoyment of the great outdoors much greater. Change that word "loot." I didn't steal from the camp. There are a few vices I don't indulge in. What I mean is that the money I made was legitimately gotten but I got it in ways that were almost like stealing they required so little effort.

The counsellors at Camp Mohawk were paid salaries that made sweat-shops look good. We were supposed to use the money we made in tips to bring it up to a decent level. Most of the campers were rich kids from New York whose parents gave us good tips at the end of the summer. I'll bet I made more that way than any of the other counsellors.

The kids' fathers almost always doubled the twenty or thirty dollars their wives told them to give me. They liked the way the camp tee shirts stretched to bursting over my prematurely lush bosom (the camp insignia which was stamped on the left breast pocket stood out prominently over the tip of my 38C. It was very noticeable there. Maybe that's why the men always noticed the camp's Latin motto and bent close to do a careful translation). I always dispensed with panties and bra when parents were visiting the camp. The men liked the way my hips rolled as I walked and the twin mounds of my buttocks jiggled with each step. The skin-tight short shorts and tee shirts I wore on those occasions made it obvious to them that I wasn't wearing any underclothing. So the fathers gave me big tips and I paid them back with a smile and an extra twitch or two to my behind as I walked away.

I keep talking about accumulating money like it was the most important thing in the world to me and at other times I've spoken of myself as liking the fine arts and things like that. It probably doesn't sound quite right. You must think I'm some kind of phony. I'm not, I just feel as Somerset Maugham does. He once said that, "Money is a sixth sense without which you can't enjoy the other five." I couldn't agree with him more.

I always liked the camp and the money I made there made it even nicer. The drawback lay in the loneliness I felt. I've always felt lonely and being at the camp where there were lots of people my own age but none I could be really friendly with made the problem worse. It was like seating a starving man in front of a table laden with delectable fruits, every one of them made of plaster. The girls were friendly and I got along well with them but I longed for one person to whom I could tell everything and who would be an individual in her own right, not like the boy-crazy adolescents who surrounded me.

All my life, it seems to me now, I've had a crush on some woman. There was never very much to it. I would just pick out a teacher or some other older woman and she would be my obssession for a few months or a year until I replaced her with someone else. I never tried to get close to my crushes. They served the purpose of giving an object to my fantasy-life and someone to model myself after and that was all I wanted from them. I would pretend to myself that I was talking to which ever one of them had top billing at the moment and it was almost as good as having her there. Almost but not quite.

The summer of my graduation from college, the period that intervened before coming to Oakwood to live with Janet, a new nurse came to work at Camp Mohawk. Her name was Karen Lerner and I thought she was the most beautiful woman in the world. It wasn't long before I had a full-blown crush on her.

She was about thirty-five, medium height, smooth boyish figure, had blue eyes and wore her blonde hair in a sophisticated chignon. I worshipped her from afar and would have been content to just keep it that way. I had done very well in the past without ever letting the women I adored know how I felt about them. I was sure that Karen hardly knew I existed. She was polite and friendly towards me but she acted the exact same way with everybody else.

Karen's room was opposite mine in the counselor's cabin. The shower was at the end of a long hall. One day I came back to the cabin early when I thought no one else would be there. I took a shower and started to run back to my room with a towel wrapped around me. Just before I reached my door I stumbled and the towel dropped off me. Before I could pick it up again, the door to the room opposite mine opened and Karen looked out to see what the noise had been. I was very embarrassed but she just laughed and looked at me in a funny way. It was strange but while she was looking at me I didn't feel uncomfortable about being naked any longer. She didn't seem embarrassed either. She seemed almost glad.

After that we became friends and she used to invite me to her room late at night when there were no patients in the infirmary that she had to stay with. We would drink bourbon out of paper cups and tell each other silly stories which we made up as we went along. I thought she was the most wonderful woman in the world.

One night I stayed in her room until nearly three o'clock in ther morning. We had had more than our usual amount to drink and the hours had passed by unnoticed. When I finally got up to leave I was a little unsteady on my feet.

"Goodnight," I said. "I'll see you tomorrow."

"Not until tomorrow? I doubt that," Karen said.

"What do you mean?"

"You'll dream about me. You do every night, don't you, Paula? I'm with you in your dreams, isn't that true?"

Abruptly I was cold sober. How did she know? I had never told her. Our conversations had always been completely impersonal.

Karen didn't wait for a reply. She came over to me and put her hands on my shoulders. "Wouldn't it be better to bring a little reality into the picture? To have me be really with you instead of just dreaming about it?"

I was trembling all over. Karen led me to the bed and sat me down on the edge. She started undressing me, my hands were shaking so badly I couldn't have done the job myself. When all my clothes were off she stood over me admiring my naked body. Then she backed away and started taking off her own clothes.

I lay back on the pillow confused and happy. Somewhere in the back of my mind I must have known what would come next but I had never consciously thought about it. I had just wanted to have Karen take me in her arms in a sterile embrace of affection. That seemed the greatest happiness to me. I closed my eyes, thinking that in a few minutes she would be lying next to me in the bed and perhaps she would put her arms around me and we could go to sleep that way.

"Why do you have your eyes closed? Don't you want to look at me?"

I opened my eyes. Karen was standing in the middle of the room. All her clothes were off. She was, if possible, even more beautiful that way. Her breasts were small and pointed, her skin smooth and inviting.

Then she was in the bed next to me and our lips were locked. I felt myself drowning in the exquisite sweetness of her kiss. Karen moved on top of me. I could feel her body matching every line and curve of mine. Her body ground rhythmically against mine, our lips kept locked together, our tongues playing the game of advance and retreat.

Karen's breath was coming in short gasps, irregular and jagged. She raised herself up on one elbow. With her free hand she cupped my breast. Smoothly she moved her hand around and around in circles. Then she placed the flat of her palm against the tip, caressing the nipple until it stood up stiffly.

"Karen," I breathed.

"What, darling?"

"I love you. Karen, Karen, I love you."

"I know you do, darling."

She lowered her head and kissed my breast. The kiss was long and infinitely sensual. Slowly she moved her lips around, teasing the nipple with her tongue. The excitement was unbearable. I felt as though I was going to burst. And yet it was so lovely to feel her hot flesh against mine and the exquisite torture of her mouth on my breast that I never wanted her to move.

There were greater pleasures in store for me though. Karen slid her hands delicately over my body. She followed with her tongue and lips where her hands had been. I could hear my own tortured breathing.

Then the tension in my body reached the point where I could bear it no longer.

"Now!" I called out.

My hands grasped at Karen's head as the flame of pleasure overwhelmed me. Far away I could hear Karen moaning in ecstacy. I could feel her body stiffening at the same moment as every muscle in mine tensed and the world and yesterday and tomorrow were swept away in the wonderous release of the moment.

After that night I slept with Karen often. I knew there was a name for what we were doing but I didn't care. Nothing could be really wrong that was so wonderful. It was so different from being with a man. All a man was interested in was thrusting his need into my body and getting his satisfaction. Their brutal hands had used my body, not played with it gently as Karen did to evoke greater and greater heights of pleasure.

Karen was so soft. Her breasts were like twin mounds of security when I laid my head between them. I adored the feminity of her body and hated the rough hardness that was men. For a month I was perfectly happy, feeling that I had come home at last.

Karen had told me about her many other lovers. I didn't care. It was only important that she wanted me now. Whatever had happened in her past didn't count, I had done lots of things I wanted forgotten too. My bubble burst one night when I found out how she really felt.

We had arranged to take the same day off. Karen had attended to the one patient in the infirmary, a young counselor named Betty, before leaving for the day. We had the whole afternoon and early evening off before we would have to return. Because there was a patient in the infirmary, Karen would have to sleep there when we returned. There was a little room off the infirmary where she stayed when she had a patient. For the past week Karen had slept there almost every night. She said that there was some sort of virus making the rounds of the camp and there was always someone staying in the infirmary who might require her attention during the night.

The nights I hadn't been with her had been torture. My body had come alive under Karen's tutelage. Now I was filled with longings which only she could satisfy. It had been days since I had lain in her arms and I was aching with yearning. Karen seemed pleased and flattered when I told her about it. She said that I could come back to the infirmary with her that night and stay with her if Betty was better.

We spent the day shopping and seeing a movie. Then we headed back toward the camp in Karen's car. Although the needle on the speedometer was hovering between forty and forty-five it seemed as if the little convertible were riding above the road on a self-made highway of speed. The twisting lakeside road wound tunnel-like under the black trees. Moonless, the sky was an inverted colander on which occasional drops of light hung suspended. The camp area itself was absolutely black save for where the car headlights assaulted here a startled rabbit, there a sleeping cabin.

There was dance music on the radio. Hesitantly, the music reached us from a New York station across the Sound, fading when we went under telephone wires, then suddenly coming through strong and clear.

Karen maneuvered the car along with the deceptively negligent ease of a driver who identifies so completely with the machine that it is as though the auto were part of her own body. Her hands rested lightly on the wheel as if she were relaxed in a chair somewhere, her eyes on the absorbing play of an open fire.

It felt as though we were being carried on twin hands of motion and sound. I glanced over at Karen's darkened profile. Her blondeness was hidden in the night's obscurity. In the dim reflection from the dashboard Karen's sharp profile, her hair blowing back in the wind, a gentle smile playing on her lips, looked a thing of beauty.

"You know, I could love someone for just this."

Karen smiled in answer.

"It's as though," I continued, "we were completely alone in a world of beauty and aliveness."

Karen sighed. "Ah, look, you realize Betty may have to stay in the infirmary. That is, it would look funny if you stayed there with me. She might tell someone about it."

Aliveness sang to the tops of the hovering trees and died. "Guesss you're right," I said, my voice heavy with disappointment.

"Hey, wait a minute, don't get all depressed. Who knows, Betty might be able to go back to her own cabin. We'll see when we get there."

A strange suspicious thought occurred to me. "But even if she does stay in the infirmary, she needn't know I'm there. There's a separate entrance to your room."

"We were talking and she fell asleep in my room. I let her stay there. Don't worry, I think I can send her back to her own cabin."

"C'mon, what's the pitch? There's something fishy about all this."

"Don't be silly, Betty's just a kid. Do you know her?"

"No, she handles the seven year olds over on the other side of the camp. I'm not even sure I've ever met her. I seldom come in contact with the counselors of the younger bunch."

"Well, Betty wasn't feeling so well this afternoon. She came to the infirmary and I looked her over. It looked like just a cold to me but she was afraid she'd pass it on to the campers so I suggested that she stay there for a while. Let's argue about it later, huh? Someone might hear us out here."

The car gave a small shudder as we passed over a concealed root. Karen slammed on the brakes just before we went into a tangle of slim white birches—their trunks intertwined like lovers looking startled and naked in the bold glare of the headlights.

"Well, we're here."

I looked around at what seemed to be a wilderness of dark trees. About twenty yards away the outlines of a small building could be dimly seen. We stumbled up to the door in the dark.

Inside, the smell of freshly-cut pine betrayed the cabin's newness. We stopped at the doorway to the bedroom, holding our breath so as not to disturb the sleeping girl on the cot.

"I'll get her up," Karen said. "She's been sleeping long enough."

She sat down on the edge of the cot. Putting her head next to the sleeping girl's she murmured, "Betty, Betty, wake up now, darling." No response. "Come on now, Betty, get up. You've slept long enough." No response.

Karen looked at me with a smile of mock defeat. "Looks like this calls for stronger measures." She gave the girl a resounding whack on her upturned rump.

The girl yelped softly as if in sleep and, turning slowly onto her back, her eyes still closed, stretched out her arms gropingly in the dark. "Karen, is that you?"

"Yes. I've brought a friend with me."

The girl snapped awake. Fumbling with the buttons on her opened pajama top she peered into the darkness. "Who? Hey, wait a minute, don't put on any lights yet. I haven't got any clothes on. Okay, now."

With the lights on I could see that the "kid" was a highly presentable woman in her early twenties. Oh brother, I thought, was I supposed to fall for this? That "kid's" slept here plenty of times … and not on the cot. Might have known Karen had something else cooking. I couldn't gripe though. We had agreed, no promises, no ties. It still hurt.

Introductions and solicitous inquiries as to her health over, Betty started to leave.

"What's your hurry?" Karen asked. "Stay with us for a while. Here, let me see if you still have a temperature." She pressed her lips to the girl's forehead. Not exactly professional procedure. "No, you seem all right." But still her arm remained around Betty's shoulders.

I was furious. I knew I ought to have expected something like this. I'd read a lot of books about lesbians and the one thing that had impressed me the most was the ephemeralness of the relationships. I knew that most people who liked their vice *versa* changed lovers often and/or were unfaithful to each other. Yet, Karen had been so affectionate. True, she had never told me she loved me. She acted as if she did. That was more important. Now she was acting as if I didn't exist and Betty was getting most of her attention.

In the dim light from the bedside lamp we talked about camp matters. My hurt and anger grew as I watched Karen almost absent-mindedly playing with Betty's hair, running her hand up and down the girl's bare arm.

At last, Betty left for her own cabin. Karen walked out to the path with her. In the still night I could hear them whispering, a stifled giggle and then the unmistakable absence of sound of a kiss.

Karen came back into the infirmary humming.

"She seems like a nice kid," I said.

"Betty? She's a darling. So good with the campers. She seems much better. Her fever's all gone."

"Amazing. Have the Mayo brothers heard about your techniques? You might revolutionize modern medicine." I hated myself for betraying my feelings that way but I couldn't help it.

Karen laughed and, sitting down on the bed beside me, pulled my head down onto her lap. "I guess I should have told you before." She stopped, then laughed again. "You know what I'm like, Paula. I've told you all about myself. This is the way I am and you should have expected that there would be someone else. I don't believe in confining myself to one person."

"But why, Karen? What do you get out of it? Besides sex, of course." I hesitated as I felt something cold twisting inside me. I chose to ignore it. "I don't understand why you waste time this way. Instead of concentrating on building a meaningful relationship with one woman, you dissipate your time and energy with many. That way you're left with nothing in the end."

"On the contrary, I'm left with a great deal. Myself." Karen stared at the opposite wall. Her eyes were motionless orbs, seeing nothing. Finally she spoke again, her voice curiously heavy. "I tried it your way once. I guess every girl does when she's first starting out. They tell me that some stay together and don't have to change. That's what they tell me but I've yet to see it for myself and I'm from Missouri. You think I'm some kind of gay nymphomaniac because you're new to the game. Ordinarily, I'd just let you find out what life is all about on the dark side of the moon by yourself. But because I am really genuinely fond of you, I'm going to try to warn you of what to expect so you won't have to find out the hard way."

Karen stopped to light a cigarette before continuing. "My first affair was with an older woman. That's a fairly typical pattern and it continues to get even more typical. I loved her very much and had good reason to believe that she loved me. We had two years together of exquisite happiness. Then she left me. It doesn't matter why. She left and the reasons could have been the ones she told me or they could have been others. Anyway, after she left I was desolated. I went completely to pieces, drinking, not able to hold a job, the whole bit. I was right out of a grade B movie. It took me another two years to pull myself out of it. When I finally did, I started looking around. I knew for sure by then that I wasn't for men so I had to see how other women like me who could only care for there own sex managed to live a homosexual life and still be happy. I observed these women and saw that the ones who put all their eggs in one basket were either alcoholics or continually teetering on the brink of suicide. The ones who played the field and got their jollies on an easy-come-easy-go basis seemed fairly content. I even found out when I talked to them that they all had had almost exactly similar experiences to mine. The pattern was so often repeated it was a classic." Karen laughed bitterly. "There's something annoying about the lack of originality fate has exercised in shaping my destiny.

"So I made up my mind, no use throwing good emotions after bad. I was going to play it cool. Luckily, I've found plenty of attractive women who were willing to accept me on those terms. I've been honest with every one of them. I've never promised them anything more than I was prepared to give them. You know that, Paula, I've always made sure that my lovers entered into a relationship with me with their eyes wide open."

"What do you really get from women, Karen? What is it that you see in young girls like Betty?"

"Enthusiasm. It doesn't matter what their primary interests are. I've been with women who were passionate poetesses and women who went wild at the sight of a Cadillac. It doesn't matter what their enthusiasm was for. I get a lot from other people's interests. It feeds my spirit to be with people who are passionately devoted to something. Each of the women I've been with had tremendous enthusiasm. Frequently the enthusiasm was for me ... and that's the best kind of all as far as I'm concerned."

I could feel myself softening. Typical, I thought, no matter what she does, I can never stay mad at her. I made a deliberate effort to keep the conversation going. "Do you think that's sufficient motivation to justify your actions?"

"I don't see where they need justification. I've got a right to be friendly with whomever I choose. People like me, can't help that. Once they get to know me better, I think I'm very good for them. All the relationships I've had with women have been fun."

"I'll bet! Especially in bed! Dammit, Karen, they weren't just casual friendships. You can't take a girl who has never been to bed with a woman before, make love to her for as long as you're both in the same place and then expect her to treat it as an interrupted friendship when you go off somewhere and pick up with someone else."

"Why not? I think you take this whole sex thing too seriously, Paula. It's just a way of getting people to relax. It's a real shortcut to getting to know people better."

Hearing the bantering tone come back into Karen's voice, I knew that the conversation had hit a dead end. There were certain areas where Karen couldn't see beyond her own proclivities.

"I just like people to feel relaxed and let themselves go with me. A little exchange of physical affection always helps that along."

"Anything you say," I said in frustration. "Let's drop the whole thing and go to sleep. You're incorrigible."

We prepared for bed in silence. When we were lying next to each other I said, "I'll miss you after this summer is over."

"I'll come to visit you," Karen murmured sleepily. "And you can spend your Thanksgiving or Christmas vacation at my place in New York if you'd like."

"Thanks, I'd like. It'll seem like ages until November. I'll miss not sleeping with you. I've gotten used to the feeling of a soft warm body next to me in the bed."

"You'll find someone to console you."

"In Oakwood?"

"Sure, in Oakwood. I know it's a small town but there's a very good chance that you'll find other gay women there. They won't be as obvious about it as they would be in some place like New York but just take your time and you'll probably meet somebody you'll like. I know someone I think you'd really go for. By a revolting coincidence whose Freudian implications we'll ignore, she's a teacher in Oakwood too. She and I had an affair many years ago. I hope you two like each other. It would be wonderful if you could get together."

I snapped awake, my ears tingling with attention like a hunting dog's. "Who is she?"

"Does Macy's tell Gimbel's?" Karen laughed. "Don't you know that one of the cardinal rules among gay women is to be discreet about using names? A good way to get yourself declared off-limits by every gal worth knowing is to start blabbing names all over the place. The only time it's permissible is when you're talking to someone who has had an affair with the same woman. The other case is with very prominent actresses who have a reputation for being gay anyway. The night after the Academy Awards are given out, half the lesbians in New York are down in the bars bragging to everybody in sight that they've been to bed with the star. Sometimes they really have but you never can be sure."

"It doesn't matter, I'll probably never meet your friend and I don't care. I've made up my mind that I'm going to become an ascetic. I should say, my mind's been made up for me. Hell of a lot of kicks I'll get in a place like Oakwood."

"You?" Karen laughed. "A sexy piece like you? That'll be the day. You'll probably start making time with your roommate two days after you get there."

"Janet? She's straight."

"Define your terms."

"You know what I mean."

"Face it," Karen said, "the definition of a straight woman is someone who has never been to bed with another woman, right? Okay, Janet's only in her early twenties. If she hasn't had a gay affair yet it doesn't prove a thing. We all have to get started sometime. I don't call a woman straight until she's sixty. Come to think of it, I change that. I knew a woman down in Florida once who lost her husband when she was sixty-two and then she took off after every young girl she could get. Nope, change my definition. You can't tell what a woman is until she's dead and it's too late for her to do anything.

"But back to this Janet chick. You seem to like her a lot. Are you sure that there isn't something significant between you two?"

I laughed. Slipping my arm under Karen's head, I cradled her like a child. "Significantly? From your point of view, apropos of big fat frienships, it's very significant. We've had some very nice intimate conversations. Friendly as all hell, I'd say."

"Bitch! You know what I mean. Are you attracted to her? Do you want to sleep with her?"

"I decline to answer on the grounds that I think that you 'take this whole sex thing too seriously'."

Karen laughed luxuriantly. "Okay, you made your point. And I won't ask any more questions if you'll tickle my back. You know, the way I like it."

"Do you always ask your women to tickle your back?"

"Uh-huh, puts me to sleep."

She rolled over onto her stomach. I propped myself up on one elbow and ran my hand gently over Karen's back. The thin stuff of her pajamas barely concealed her ripples of pleasure that were going through her body. I fought hard to think about other things as I tickled Karen's back. The pain of finding Betty in her bed earlier in the evening was still too fresh. I fought against having the contact with Karen's body awaken desire in me. I wanted time to myself to think before I again surrendered myself to her.

Karen's sun-streaked yellow hair was a fragrant mass close to my face as I moved my hand up her neck to the hairline, down along the indentation of her spine, along the soft flesh below her waist. I raised her pajama top. Karen gave a moan of exaggerated bliss as my cool fingers caressed her warm skin.

Karen's hair brushed my face as I rocked gently with the movement of my hand. Hypnotically I stared at the smooth skin beneath my hand which looked a pale cold blue in the moonlight. I bent down and ran my tongue slowly up the length of Karen's spine. She shivered and gasped.

Turning on her back, she caught me in her arms and pulled me down on top of her. Our lips met. Slowly, as if tasting an exquisite fruit, Karen moved her mouth against mine. The tip of her tongue caressed the sensitive line of my mouth. Then, hungrily. I sucked her tongue into my own mouth. Karen's body began to move rhythmically against mine.

Suddenly, I broke away. "This is wrong. Let's stop it here."

Karen's voice was like purring, her mouth against my neck. "I think it's very right."

"What about Betty?"

"She's asleep by now in her own cabin. What about her?"

"This isn't being fair to her."

"She needn't know about it. Besides, she knows that you're one of my dearest friends. She wouldn't want me to be unfriendly."

I started to laugh but my laugh turned to a gasp as Karen ripped open my pajama top and bit softly into my breast, her tongue teasing the pliant nipple.

"Oh, no, baby, no. Baby, baby, oh ... "

At the end of the summer Karen returned to New York. I had no illusions left about her after that night in the infirmary. I knew that I was only a plaything to her, that my love was all one-sided. It didn't matter. Lying on the couch that night and thinking about Karen I thought that I probably ought to curse the day I met her but no matter how long she kept me waiting, no matter how many begging letters I had to send her, no matter what might happen between us, I'd always be hers. Karen Lerner taught me how to be happy and how to be sad ... and who knows which has the sweeter flavor?

I would never be the same after that summer with Karen. Good or bad she taught me to know myself for what I am. That's why I refused to sleep in the other twin bed with Janet. There were two dangers in it. How did I know that I might not call out Karen's name in my sleep? It would be a fine thing if Janet heard me whispering terms of endearment to a woman. Also, I was afraid that Karen's insight had more than a little basis in truth. I did find Janet attractive. Suppose I should find her nearness in the bedroom too exciting and attempt to make love to her? Janet would wake up and be horrified. There I'd be with egg on my face and an ache in my loins that sweet innocent young Janet could never understand, would find disgusting.

No, I could get too much out of just living with Janet and being her friend to risk ruining the whole thing. If some day she should come to want me as I wanted her ... well, that would be a different story. I drifted off to sleep knowing that I loved Karen thoroughly and completely with all my heart and soul and would probably continue to love her that way until Janet would allow me to give my love to her.

CHAPTER THREE

We went to the school the next day. There were a thousand and one details we had to take care of before classes started the following morning. There would be no time then to inventory supplies, etc.

I was nervous as a cat but I tried not to show it because I didn't want Janet to pick up my mood and get the shakes herself. She let me know that she felt the same way and also was aware of what I was going through just before we parted in the corridor to go to our separate rooms. Janet seized my hand in a convulsive clasp of understanding and reassurance before parting. Her room was directly opposite mine and I could see into it through the opened door. We walked to our desks then turned and smiled at each other before turning our attention to the task at hand.

My first impression of my classroom was that it was too big. Too big for the size class we had been told was ideal in college. How would I get to know the names, the personalities, the needs of all the children who tomorrow would fill those seats? Discouraged and not a little frightened by the eminence of something I had planned on all my life and spent the last four years preparing for, I set about taking care of the little details that I wouldn't have time for in the morning.

The blackboards hadn't been washed since last term and on them were the half-completed sentences, the meaningless words that had been part of someone else's idea of how to handle this job. Perhaps my predecessor had been more capable than I and had established a reputation for orderly classrooms and alert pupils that I would be judged against.

I glance over into Janet's room. Obviously, she was feeling as bad as I was. She was sitting at her desk with her head in her hands. Discouragement showed in the weary slump of her shoulders.

Just then a woman entered her room and stood looking down at her for a moment before speaking.

"Giving up already?"

The soft voice behind her startled Janet out of her reverie. Miss Winsor, principal of the Oakwood Elementary School, was standing beside her desk, smiling down at her kindly.

Helen Winsor bore little resemblance to the sterotype of an elementary school principal. She was tall and thin with a body like that of a dancer. Her face had nothing of commercial beauty in it but a suggestion of character was there which earned her the attention and devotion of both pupils and teachers on first meeting. Her hair was completely white but the healthy flush on her cheeks, innocent of make-up, and the young aliveness of her movements indicated that her hair had lost its color prematurely.

I could see and hear clearly everything in the room across the hall. I remained motionless at my desk, hoping not to be noticed.

Miss Winsor was wearing a thin black jumper which emphasized her slimness and brought out the whiteness of her hair. The dress would have been too youthful had not the swelling bodice indicated a body underneath that demanded the freedom of free-swinging clothes, the outspokeness of Junior fashions.

"I ... I was just making plans for my first class," Janet stammered as she hastened to her feet.

The sudden freezing of the smile on Helen Winsor's face brought Janet to abrupt awareness of her own appearance. Presuming that we would be the only ones at the school that day we had dressed casually. Janet was wearing shorts and a low-cut summer blouse. Against the white of her shorts her tanned legs looked flawlessly warm, the glow of warm skin tones against pale clothing emphasized the smooth brown of her thighs, the rounded insouciance of a girl about to enter womanhood.

"We'll meet in my office tomorrow at eight," Miss Winsor said stiffly and, turning on her heel, walked hastily out of the room.

Janet came rushing across the hall into my room. She was upset about the horrible impression she was sure she had made on Miss Winsor.

"Oh Lord, Paula," Janet wailed, "why couldn't I have taken the time to put on a skirt? What kind of a kid must she take me for?"

"I woudn't worry about it. She might not be as displeased as you think."

I know damned well Helen Winsor was far from displeased by what she had seen! I couldn't explain that to Janet, though. How could I tell her that I knew our principal's embarrassment had not come out of prudery? The look on her face had been as clear as crystal to me. My little roommate had herself a female admirer. Fancy that. I knew what Janet would think if I told her what I thought. She would immediately jump to the conclusion that it takes one to know one and my particular inverted cat would be out of the bag.

Helen Winsor's—hell, from now on I'm just going to call her Helen—after all, by this point in my narrative I was pretty damn sure that she was a member of the same twilight sorority as I was and that made us some sort of crazy sisters, didn't it? Whoops, I mean queer sisters.

Anyway, Helen's attentions to Janet had made me a little jealous. That night I decided not to sleep in the living room again. I was going to share the bedroom with Janet. You might call it establishing squatter's rights.

I bathed first and was in bed when Janet came out of the shower. She was naked. She walked unconcernedly over to the dresser and stood looking in the mirror. I laid in bed pretending to be asleep. My eyes were half-closed so that they would appear to be completely shut. Actually, I was observing Janet minutely.

Naked she was more fully developed than I had expected. There was a lush ripeness to her body. It was the body of a fully matured woman. The body of a woman who was made to be loved.

Janet clasped her hands above her head and stretched in a long lazy yawn. The gesture pulled her breasts taut. She relaxed down again with the easy grace of a cat.

Janet paced back and forth, picking up articles of clothing which were lying around and hanging them up in the closet. I watched the swing of her lush buttocks. God, she was desirable.

No, I told myself, not yet anyway. Maybe not ever. I fought hard to push down the raging fire which the sight of Janet's body had aroused in me. I grabbed hunks of the sheet in my sweating palms, digging my nails furiously into the cloth balls. I must control myself. Janet must not know how I feel.

I was disgusted with myself. What kind of a freak was I? It had only been a little over a week since I had last been with Karen and I was horny as all hell already. A lascivious lesbian. What next? Hell of a good school teacher I'd make if I couldn't think of anything except sex. I'd end up taking my students out to the cloakroom to have "conferences" with them. Not all my students, just the girls. Oh great, a gay Blanche DuBois.

That night again I didn't get much sleep. The next morning I was facing my first class and that, coupled with the nearly sleepless night, made me so tense I wanted to scream.

It was all right, though. As soon as I got in front of the class my nervousness left me. It was like having stage fright. Most performers experience some form of stage fright all through their careers. Once they get out on the stage the feeling leaves them and they're okay. That's the way I was. My mind was so occupied with managing my class that I had no time in which to become nervous.

Things began settling into an easy rhythm. Living with Janet was fun. She was easy to talk to and I felt comfortable with her. We were both very busy composing lesson plans for the months ahead and only had time for conversation over dinner.

I liked being with Janet most of time. It was only at night that it became torture. Each night I arranged it so that Janet would already be asleep by the time I entered the bedroom. Never again did I want to experience the delicious torture of seeing her naked before me.

So I stayed in the living room and wrote letters to Karen while Janet prepared for bed. They were long passionate letters full of pleading. I knew that Karen couldn't leave her job and come to Oakwood to see me. Yet, I implored her to find a way to hold me again in her arms. If only she would quench the raging desires within me so that I could really regard Janet as the friend she believed me to be.

And because I knew that my letters were mostly lies, I tore most of them up and threw them away. Who was I kidding? Karen knew as well as I did that New York was near enough to Oakwood for me to visit her on a weekend if I really wanted to. I wanted Karen to make love to me yet I was unwilling to part from Janet even for a few days.

Each night I would look over at Janet sleeping in the bed next to mine and long to grasp her to me. She was so near and yet so far away. How I ached to run my hands over her lush flesh!

The second week of school was, if anything, even more frightening than the first had been. The children had gotten over their initial excitement and were already beginning to settle down into cliques. Their attention was no longer solely on themselves and their classmates. They were ready now to appraise their new teachers.

I stood before my class thinking that never before had I felt the full power of unreasoning group hostility. What is it, I wondered, that makes them dislike me so much? What have I done to them? I'm here to help them. I tried every technique I could remember from my college training to bring the class into harmony, but they resisted me.

The restless movements of the class every time I turned my back and the trance-like inanimate quality of their expressions when I faced them soon had me on the edge of panic. Desperately I tried to show them that I was their friend. They weren't buying it.

There was one little girl in the fifth row who looked more friendly than the rest of them. She was smaller than the others, her smallness emphasized by the big blue bow in her fluffy corn-colored hair.

I went over to her desk and knelt down beside the little girl. My head was on a level with her young blonde one. I leaned close to her and, carefully keeping my voice even and cheerful, asked, "Would you like to come to the front of the room with me and tell the class what you did this summer?"

The little girl smiled sweetly and lisped, "Oh, Miss Harmon, I didn't do *anything* this summer."

There was a subdued tittering through the classroom that grew in volume as I continued to squat beside the little girl. Soon the whole class was laughing openly at my discomfort.

The little girl kept on smiling and shaking the blue satin bow. "I'm sorry, Miss Harmon. Would you like me to do something else for you?" she asked in a lisping voice of such saccharine sweetness that compared with her Shirley Temple would sound like Dietrich.

My face was burning beet red as I hastily got to my feet. I started walking back toward the front of the classroom, in complete confusion. The roar of laughter in the classroom reached a crescendo.

The little girl was running after me, pleading with me through chokes of laughter, "Miss Harmon, my ribbon. You've caught my ribbon."

The huge bow had caught on a button of my blouse and, as I rose, had come undone and was now trailing behind me like a heraldic pennant. I ripped it loose and flung it behind me to the little girl. Then I put my hands over my face and ran out of the classroom, crying.

The Teachers' Lounge was at the end of the hall, behind a frosted glass door. I stumbled over someone as I flung myself through the doorway and down onto a couch to bury my head in my arms and sob.

"Hey," I heard a man's voice saying, "the way you came at me you'd think you were one of my pupils I'd just flunked." Pause. "Lady, methinks thou art distressed."

"Oh," I sobbed, burying myself deeper into a pillow, "what am I going to do? They hate me already and they don't even know me. They won't even give me a chance."

"You mean the kids in your class? Don't let them get you. They do that to every new teacher. They're just trying to see how much you can take. Let them know that they can break you down and you've lost them forever. It's rough, I know. I'll never forget my first month of teaching. It taught me a valuable lesson, though. Every year since then I've been prepared for the little monsters. It's gotten to be like part of a ritual. If I ever got a class that didn't try its damndest to make a monkey out of me I wouldn't know what to do with them. Be prepared for it, every year you're going to face a new class that's going to put you through the same trial by fire. It's not so bad once you get used to it. You find that kids have a limited bag of tricks and in time you come to anticipate them all and stop them before they start."

I had stopped crying. What he said was making sense. The horrible confusion was leaving me.

"Look," he continued, "remember how it was when you were their age? They're confronted with a new person whom they don't know anything about at all and told that she'll be in a position of authority over them. For the next ten months they're going to have to listen to you, do what you say, care how you feel about them. It's frightening and they want to make sure that you're the person to handle the job. They want you to be strong so that they can rely on you not to mislead them. If they can prove that you're weak, well, then there's no reason for them to try to win your approval. It won't matter if they can't grasp the intricacies of long division if they can upset you by just pretending to be thick in the head."

"You mean," I said, "that if I'm going to be a sort of substitute for their parents when they're away from home that I've got to be a mixture of Superman, Florence Nightingale and Peewee Reese or they won't have any respect for me?"

"Exactly. That is, up to a point. I know the junk they're handing out in Educational Psych courses these days. You've most likely been taught that you should meet your pupils on their own level. Teachers are no longer supposed to be remote figures of authority. You've been told that the best atmosphere for learning is one in which the teacher is looked upon as a friend. All that's fine. But there's a time for that when they know who is boss and they're not still confused as to just what you're doing there. It's tough to be a kid. And nobody wants to put their trust in someone who breaks down under the slightest stress."

I sat up on the couch and looked at the young man standing before me. He was tall—about six feet—slim and pleasant looking without being handsome. His features were well formed: a small, soft-looking mouth, straight nose, smooth dark skin, light brown curly hair. The details were all right but put them all together and something was wrong. There was a tension about him that at first made me think he was older than he was. As I got around to noticing his clothing I realized that he was really a young man who appeared older because he had about him an aura of premature maturity, as if he had seen too much too soon to want to remain young. He was wearing a casual tweed suit, wide-spread collar, blue and silver tie, cork-soled shoes. Not exactly an Esquire fashion plate, more like all the items in his outfit had been Christmas presents from different sources.

He grinned. "My name's Frank. Frank Yellen. I'm 29, unattached, kind to animals and free this evening if you are. Incidentally, I teach fifth grade in my off hours when I'm not counseling damsels in distress."

I smiled and offered my hand to him. "Paula Harmon, Frank, prize idiot of the ranks of second grade teachers in these here parts, over 21 and free as a bird—a dodo, that is."

I was laughing now. I knew that the tears in the corners of my eyes were brightening the sparkle in my eyes as I stood with my head titled back meeting Frank's admiring stare.

"Lady, this looks like it's going to be quite a year."

He seemed like a nice guy. I don't accept dates with nice guys. I'm for women. So why had I agreed to go out with him? For one thing, I knew I'd have to protect my reputation by dating someone. I had to be seen with men or somebody might get the wrong idea, which in my case was the right idea.

There was something else. I didn't want to be a lesbian. Not really. I'd have to have been out of my mind to deliberately want to spend the rest of my life in the shadows. I loved Karen but that hadn't proved much. Lots of women have sex with a member of their own sex when they're young and then they grow up to live completely normal lives, forgetting all about it as anything more than a childish phase in their lives. If you don't believe me, read the Kinsey Report.

Karen's pessimism had affected me too. I didn't want to spend the rest of my life trying to outguess my lover. According to Karen, homosexual women played a constant game of seeing who would do the rejecting first. Sounded pretty dismal to me.

Okay, so I had never liked going to bed with a man. The ecstacy I knew in Karen's arms had never come to me when I was with a man. That still didn't prove that I was abnormal. It was perfectly logical in view of my background. It was because of his need for sex that my father was unable to be a proper parent to me. Naturally, I had grown up with a warped attitude toward sex. There was still the possibility that I'd get over his influence.

Understand me, I'm not chicken. If I had been sure at the time that I was really gay I would have accepted it. I wouldn't have tried to prove something to myself by going out with Frank Yellen. There are far worse things than being a lesbian. One of them is not being anything.

Frank could come in handy for another reason. I had to do something to alleviate the crying need for sexual release that was threatening to overpower my good sense. If that happened I would make a pass at Janet. No, that must not happen unless she comes to me. I would do anything, even sleep with a man, to prevent myself from putting our friendship in jeopardy.

The door to the lounge opened and Janet came rushing up to me and put her arms around my shoulders.

"You poor kid. What happened. I saw you running down the hall but I couldn't come in here until I had adjourned my class for lunch."

I turned toward Frank. "Janet, I'd like you to meet Frank Yellen. Frank, my roommate, Janet Coxe."

"Hi," Janet said, "Maybe you'll tell me what's been going on."

"It's nothing, Jan," I said. "I just let the kids get on my nerves. I'll tell you all about it when we get home tonight."

"Hey," Frank interjected, "I've got a great idea. Paula and I have a date this evening, Janet. Maybe you'd like to join us. My friend Bud's a swell guy. I'm sure you two would get on great together."

Janet's eyes became hard. "No, Mr. Yellen, thank you very much but I have work to do."

"Well, some other time," Frank stammered in confusion. "Paula, shall I pick you up at seven?"

"Fine, Frank, see you then."

As soon as Frank had left the room, Janet turned angrily to me. "Who is he?"

"I just met him now. He teaches fifth grade here. I think he's very nice. Don't you, Janet?"

"Charming! Just an ever-living doll! What does he want with you?"

"Jan, what's the matter with you? He asked me to go out with him this evening and I accepted. What's wrong with that?"

"And what am I supposed to do? Sit home and watch the clock to make sure that you get home in time to get your beauty sleep?"

"He asked you to join us. If you don't want to stay home why don't you come along? It'll probably be fun."

"Fun!" Janet spat out. "Is that your idea of fun? To trade a dinner or a movie for the right to have some man paw all over your body?"

Then I began to understand. Janet was jealous! She was no prude. Janet had already told me that she wasn't a virgin and she knew that I wasn't. Ordinarily, she would have been glad for the opportunity to meet new men. This was different. Janet was flipping because she didn't like to think that someone else might touch me. Fancy that! It was a good sign for the future but it might not work out in the end. Remember what they say about one swallow not making a Spring.

I calmed Janet down. When she had collected herself, she admitted that she had been unreasonable. She even admitted that she'd like to meet Frank's friend Bud.

"Come on," she said. "Let's go to the cafeteria and have lunch. Maybe Frank will be there. I'd like to apologize to him. If I haven't offended him too much already maybe he'll still be able to arrange that date for me."

It would be good for Jan to have a date. I wasn't concerned about her getting involved with any man. What worried me was Helen Winsor. She hadn't made any overt gestures as yet but I knew she was attracted to Janet. I would have real competition from that corner.

Frank arranged the double date. We would all stay together for the evening. That was a good idea. That way I'd be around to make sure that Bud didn't try to horn in on my territory.

CHAPTER FOUR

Frank's friend Bud turned out to be a very nice guy. He was a high school biology teacher who looked more like a football coach. Tall, broad-shouldered, with a face that had all the ingredients to make it incredibly handsome if it didn't look as if somebody had stepped on it. Still, he was good to look at. Ordinarily I don't like pretty men, I can't believe they're quite real, they look like the men who advertise expensive custom-made shirts. I always get the feeling that someone has wound them up so that they can walk and talk like ordinary mortals and, when the spring runs down, they'll disappear back between the covers of a magazine.

I liked Bud's looks though. He was so totally unaware of his extraordinary attractiveness that I couldn't help but forgive him for being more beautiful than any man was ever meant to be.

He was a personality kid too. It's hard to pin down exactly what it was about Bud that made him so likeable. He wasn't especially witty or intelligent. What made him so nice to be with was his open friendly manner. He was warm and generous and made the rest of us feel that he really liked us.

That's a great gift, being able to communicate warmth. Most people act as if they're indifferent to everybody else except maybe the one person they love. Bud was ready to give all degrees of affection from friendship to romantic love. In a way, I wish he hadn't been so damned appealing. It would have made it a lot easier if I could have hated him for the way Janet went for him.

The four of us went out together many times. It was fun and it gave me the opportunity to gauge just how much Janet really cared for Bud. She didn't give me too much reason to be jealous. Of course, we would kiss the men goodnight in the car at the end of each evening. Then, as Frank was holding me in his arms, I would open my eyes to watch the other couple. It hurt to see someone else making love to Janet. At the same time I got a strange kind of a thrill out of watching them. I would imagine that it was I who was holding Janet in my arms as Bud really was, my lips and not his that were locked with hers.

Frank was nice too. I didn't like his being so nice. I wouldn't have felt as guilty as I did about exploiting him if he had been an aggressive bore like most men. Instead, he was tender and affectionate with me and so damned passive I could have kicked him. He let me know that he found me sexually attractive but he never pushed it. He tried to be too understanding. Frank knew that many women are easily put off by masculine abruptness so he led up to a more intimate relationship cautiously, waiting for me to come to him. Sometimes I felt like I wanted him and other times I didn't. Poor sap Frank was never demanding enough to help me make up my mind. We wasted a lot of time because of his misplaced consideration.

Maybe we never would have gotten together if Helen Winsor hadn't been such a good school principal. Helen was very strong for the latest techniques in child guidance. She made it a point to confer with each teacher not only about academic performances but also about any case of psychological maladjustment that came up.

One of the little boys in Janet's class still wet his pants. Janet and Helen were conferring about him. It was a routine conference and it was also routine that they were going to discuss the boy over dinner before going to see his parents. That was one of Helen's little brainstorms, she preferred meeting with the new teachers in a restaurant instead of her office at the school. It made everything so much less formal and so much easier for them to get acquainted with each other.

There was absolutely nothing about the arrangement that I could logically object to. That didn't stop me from wanting to throw a tantrum when I heard about it. I lost my head at the idea of the two of them spending time alone together. Reason told me that it was going to be an impersonal meeting. Yet, I had seen the way Helen looked at Janet, I knew she was attracted to her. There was no guarantee of what the evening could turn into. It was unlikely that Helen would make a pass at Janet. A conversation that could include undisciplined bladders and seduction would be a funny one. Very funny. Pardon me while I laugh up a bucketful.

It got worse after Janet left the house to meet Helen. I couldn't stop myself from imagining them in all sorts of positions. It was crazy of course. Even if Helen were to use their meeting to make a play for Janet it was unlikely that they'd go to bed right away. I couldn't help myself though. The torture of picturing Janet writhing with passion in Helen's arms wouldn't stop. I had to do something, see someone, get out of that apartment.

I called Frank and asked him to go for a walk with me. We chose a country road that twisted through silent tobacco fields on its way to Hartford. There was hardly any traffic, just an occasional car that speeded past us leaving a vacuum of light and sound in its wake.

Frank was unusually quiet. I was grateful because I didn't want to talk. I couldn't have made intelligent conversation. My mind was a seething mass of anguished jealousy. I had to do something. The torment in my mind was affecting me physically. I was desperate for release.

"Let's rest a while here. I'm winded." My voice sounded queer. It was high and tight and charged with an aggressive defiance that dared him to discern my real reason for stopping.

Frank glanced at me quickly, startled. "Oh," he said, and then smiling slowly, "Let's."

We walked back from the road about thirty yards to where a small group of pines formed an odorous grove. The needles were soft under us as we sat, our bodies touching at the shoulders only.

I moved closer to Frank. He sat immobile, staring out at the surrounding darkness. I reached up and grasped his head in my hands, pulled it down and kissed him hard.

"Thanks," Frank said when I released him, "If you had to do that, I'm glad that I'm the one you picked."

"What do you mean?"

"Paula, I think it's about time you leveled with me. Don't worry nothing will change, I'll still be your friend. Now, tell me, how long have you been in love with Janet?"

I was thankful for the darkness, Frank couldn't see the red flush creeping up my face. I felt helpless and embarrassed and grateful. My throat felt dry, as if I couldn't speak. Nervous perspiration was making my hands soaking wet.

"How do you know?"

"I've been watching you. I've seen the way you act when we're all together. The way you look at Janet after you've said something clever to see if she appreciated it. The way you watch her when she's dancing with Bud. You look at her body in graceful motion and an expression of desperate hunger comes to your eyes. And, Paula, when you're kissing me goodnight, a normal woman wouldn't be watching another couple at that time."

The earth didn't open up and swallow me so I knew that silent prayers weren't going to help me.

"Janet must never know," I said.

"Most likely she doesn't. Not unless you've done something to tip her off."

"Never! I've never even touched her, Frank."

"Must be hell for you, living with her and having to pretend the way you do."

There was so much compassion in his voice that I felt like crying. For myself because I loved and must hide my love. For

Frank because he was so kind and sincere and he got stuck with a bad apple like me instead of a woman who could love him as he deserved to be loved. For the world because there were so many people like us who had too much love to give and had to go through life with their hearts held in their outstretched hands like beggars in an impoverished country.

"Janet likes you," Frank said softly.

"Not the way I want her to. Not the only way that would release me from the hell of the life I've been living."

"I wouldn't be too sure about that."

"You mean .. ?" For a moment I was speechless with joyous hope. "Frank, do you think it would be alright if I let her know how I felt? She wouldn't be horrified or disgusted or anything like that?"

"I doubt it. Not Janet." His voice became sad. "Watch yourself, Paula. Don't let yourself get hurt too much. Give her your body if and when she seems to want it. But keep some part of yourself separate from her. You may need it later when she's gone."

"You don't understand, Frank. I want to give myself to Janet completely. I want to have the gay equivalent of a marriage with her. Forever."

"That's what you want but I doubt if that's what Janet would want. Paula, you're quite a case. You're hard and cynical on the surface and inside you're as lost and vulnerable as a child. Janet's not like you. She's got a terrific drive for self-preservation. She's capable of doing almost anything for kicks without it touching her deeply. You're the kind who does things and then feels guilty about them. Janet leaves the scene of the crime without a backward glance."

I couldn't believe him. I didn't want to believe him. I was sure that jealousy had distorted his understanding of Janet.

"Come on, Frank. You don't really think that Janet would go to bed with me just for kicks."

"Yes, I do mean that. And she's entirely capable of leaving you afterward."

"What about me?" I laughed. "Who knows, I might just be going through some sort of phase. Maybe I'll change and go for the marriage and kids bit."

"I wish you would. I had a few thoughts along that line about you at first. I gave them up when I realized the truth. You're gay, Paula. And you're going to spend the rest of your life hunting for a woman with whom to share your life."

It was too much like Karen's prediction. Frank was condemning me to a life of futility and heartbreak. A surge of anger flooded through me. I felt like shouting obscenities at him.

"I'm quite capable of loving a man," I said through clenched teeth.

"No you're not. Face it. It will make things a lot easier in the long run for you if you do."

"I'll prove it to you."

I knelt in front of him. Frank started to speak. I silenced him by putting my lips against his and kissing him in a hard long kiss of passion, my mouth grinding against his.

My nails were digging into the thick muscles of his shoulders. Roughly, Frank reached up and tore them away.

"Stop this," he breathed, trying to pull his mouth away from mine.

It was too late. I couldn't stop. The long imprisoned need within me was crying for release. I caressed his body, feeling the surging urgency that gave the lie to Frank's protests.

His hands were on my chest. Weakly, his strength drained by desire, he attempted to push me away. I pushed his hands down until they were on my breasts. Frank didn't fight me any more. He lay passive and aching with the need that was mine also.

I opened my blouse and thrust his hands inside. Frank moaned low in his throat and then he was kneading my bare breasts. His rough grasp sent shocks of excitement through me. Frank pulled me down on top of him and placed his lips against my rigid nipples. A wild current of tempestuous excitement carried me along to a point of intolerable intensity.

Holding me tight against him, Frank rolled over. The pine needles were a soft cushion beneath us as we devoured each other's body.

We lay side by side together for a long time afterward, gazing at the stars in the silence of satiation.

The awful torment of my futile passion for Janet was quieted. No longer did my body ache with desire. Only my mind and heart continued longing for the peace of Janet's embrace.

My desperate experiment with Frank turned out to be a flash in the pan. The only good thing that came from it I could have accomplished without him. Not as well, I admit.

The Oakwood Elementary School was closed for a week for Thanksgiving vacation. Janet went home for the week. She was anxious to spend the time with her family. I wasn't. Mom would have been hurt if I hadn't at least put in an appearance so I went home for three days and then lit out for New York City and Karen.

You can't blame me for wanting to get out of that house as soon as I could. The three days I spent there were idyllic, a typical All-American scene, right out of an Andy Hardy movie.

My Father came sloshing into the house on the first night of my visit. He looked at me through bloodshot eyes and mumbled, "Hi. Haven't seen much of you lately. Where you been keeping yourself?" Then he stumbled up the stairs to bed, not waiting for my reply. The bastard didn't even know that I wasn't living there anymore. I had been gone since the first of September and he hadn't even noticed.

Oh well, I had come to visit my mother, not him. Mom tried her best to give me a royal welcome. It was a royal drag. She was so damned glad to see me it was pitiful. It was nice to be deluged with so much affection but Mom's reaction was excessive because she needed me to relieve her constant loneliness. All the time I was with her she kept putting on a show of good cheer. As if I didn't know how she really felt! It tore at my guts to watch my mother playing the suburban Pagliacci.

Man, was I glad to get out of there! I felt so much pity for Mom that it was driving me nuts. I was the only human being in this whole lousy world who gave a damn what happened to her and I was powerless to help her. As long as she continued living in Barrington with my father her life would be an unrelieved misery. She could have lived with me. I would have been overjoyed at the opportunity to do something for her. Talk to my mother, talk to a wall. She wouldn't even consider leaving my father.

By the time the train pulled into Grand Central Station in New York I had repressed my anguished pity for Mom. It was a technique I had learned years before because I had to. I couldn't keep brooding over a situation I could do nothing about. I still felt sorry for her, I always did. There's a difference, however, between wanting to smash your fist into a wall out of frustration and melancholic reflection.

Karen had invited me to stay in her apartment. I got into New York in the early afternoon. Karen didn't get off her job until six. She had sent me a duplicate key to her apartment but I didn't feel like going up there and being all by my lonesome so I checked my suitcase and went for a long walk.

Karen's apartment was on West 11th Street near Sixth Avenue in Greenwich Village. That gave me an excuse to walk around the Village.

It wasn't my first trip to New York. Barrington is only one hundred miles away from the City so it was no big deal for a group of us from school to run down to New York for a week-end. We always made like tourists (which we were) and dug the museums in the afternoons and the sucker trap niteclubs at night. Of course we had given the Village a look-see. Like the hicks we were we went to all the places where the local residents wouldn't be caught dead.

Once I went with three other girls to a queer niteclub. I use the word "queer" to distinguish that place from a gay bar. The only homosexuals you ever find in those queer joints are hired to give the tourists a thrill. There was a floor show that consisted of stupid songs and jokes about homosexuality. All the performers were transvestites. Some of the faggots looked gorgeous dressed up as women but the women who were wearing drag looked like they belonged on a farm. I found the place offensive, vulgar, in bad taste and I enjoyed myself hugely. That was long before I suspected that I had anything in common with the inverted exhibitionists who were the performers.

This time I was out to view the Village in a different way. I wanted to take in the scene sans cover-charge. Within ten minutes I had fallen in love with the oldworld charm of the Village. I got a kick out of seeing girls who were obviously lesbians all over the place but the wonderful little jewelry and leather shops were what sold me on the place. There was nothing like those stores in my part of the country.

It was a beautiful, crisp November day. I walked for hours, following my nose (slightly to the left). I didn't dare go into any of the stores because, if I had, I would have gone stark staring mad buying everything in sight. I didn't have that kind of loot so I had to content myself with pressing my nose against the store windows like a kid drooling over a window display in a bakery.

There were a pair of silver earrings on display in one of the shops that I really flipped for. I must have stood in front of that window for twenty minutes at least imagining how those earrings would look on Janet and then I would picture Karen wearing them. Speak of ambivalence! I finally decided where my loyalties lay by buying the earrings for myself. They set me back a much-needed twenty bucks but they were worth it. They were beautiful, exotic, original and if I ever dared wear them in Oakwood I would have been run out of town as a subversive. Great place that Oakwood ... for trees.

Somehow I wound up on MacDougal Street near Bleeker at six-thirty. I had no idea of what route had taken me there and less of how to get back. I telephoned Karen at her apartment to get directions.

The voice on the other end of the wire wasn't Karen's. It sounded familiar but I couldn't place it. That was odd, I knew no one else in New York.

The unidentified woman informed me that Karen was taking a shower and would I like to leave a message.

I was in the midst of explaining my predicament when I heard Karen in the background asking who was calling. I gave the strange woman my name.

There was a small gasp on the other end of the wire, then, "Paula! Of course, I recognized the voice but I wasn't sure. This is Helen, dear."

"Dear" no less. And "Helen." She had never encouraged me to use her first name around Oakwood. The old girl was obviously suffering from Manhattan madness.

We made with the exclamations of surprise back and forth for a while. Then Helen told me how to get back to the 14th Street subway station where I had checked my suitcase and how to get to Karen's apartment from there.

I listened to Helen's instructions very carefully and then, as soon as I hung up the phone, couldn't remember a word she had said. I always do that. Tell me how to get somewhere and I'll listen like I was hearing the Sermon on the Mount for the first time. Two minutes later I can't recall whether I was told to take a left on Sixth Avenue or follow Sixth Avenue to Left Street. In one head and out the other.

I solved my problem by taking a taxi. Let the driver worry about how to get there. Stupidity is no disadvantage if you know how to pick other people's brains.

I got out of the taxi on 11th Street. I had never seen Karen's apartment before so I cased the neighborhood first. It was a nice street with comfortable old brownstone buildings and lots of trees. It was quiet and clean for New York.

The building where Karen lived was a three-story job that had originally been a townhouse. Now it was chopped up into apartments. Karen had a floor-through on the top floor. I rang the downstairs bell and there was an answering buzz which released the lock on the door.

Lugging that suitcase up three flights of steep stairs was no joke. I had packed so much stuff into it that it seemed to weigh a ton. All the way up the stairs I kept banging my knees on that damned suitcase. That wasn't all that was bugging me. Ever since our phone conversation I had been annoyed about Helen being in Karen's apartment. What the hell was she doing there?

One thing I now knew for sure. Helen was the schoolteacher friend from Oakwood that Karen had told me about last summer. Karen had said that she thought Helen (unnamed at the time) and I would like each other. Guess again, cutie. I never have cared for old bags and Miss Winsor was no exception. She was my boss and that made for two strikes against her before she even started. And having eyes for Janet didn't endear her to me any more. Helen was threatening to become a significant factor in my life. The crowning touch was finding her in Karen's apartment when I hadn't expected to. I couldn't have expected Karen to have had the courtesy to tell me that Helen would be there. She wasn't the sort to think about doing something nice and simple like that. It would be like expecting a pigeon to be particular about who he aims at.

Helen opened the door for me. I could tell right away from the tension in the air that there had been a battle. Bet Helen gave Karen hell for not telling her ahead of time that I was expected.

Karen shouted to me from the kitchen that she was fixing up a batch of martinis and would be with me in a minute. I grunted a reply and sank exhausted into a chair and looked around me.

Karen's apartment was loaded with charm. The living room in which I was sitting was a huge rectangle with one whole wall of windows facing south onto the street. The furnishings were an unselfconscious combination of modern and traditional. The chief decoration was books—on shelves along the walls, in book-cases, stacked on the floor in disorderly piles. Against the stark serenity of the white walls, a bright red rug flamed, seeming to reach up toward the far wall which was covered entirely with drapes dyed the same color. The effect (and there was lots of it) was one of individualism at war with itself.

Karen brought out the pitcher of martinis. The three of us sat around getting politely loaded and making chit-chat. The scene reminded me of the opening scene in *Macbeth*. Helen and I made like we were glad to see each other and Karen blissfully ignored the consequences of her colossal goof. After a little while Helen and I relaxed and started talking to each other as if we were really human beings. I couldn't blame Helen for feeling uncomfortable at first. If I were in her position I wouldn't have liked any of the teachers in my school to find out that their principal was gay in that way.

Three martinis and I was beginning to think that maybe Helen wasn't so bad. I damn near fell in love with her when she announced that she had to leave because her hostess was expect-ing her. She was staying with some gal named Sandra Munson and had just been visiting Karen for a couple of hours. That was just ducky with me. Karen was looking quite delectable in tight black toreador pants and silk shirt and I was having thoughts about her that didn't include a third party. We made arrange-ments for all four of us (Sandra included) to meet later in the evening at a gay bar and Helen left.

I was starving and since Karen had olives as the only solid food in her kitchen, we went out to a restaurant for dinner. I ate dinner and watched the floorshow. It was a private performance for me only. Karen put on a great show with sexy looks and dia-logue that was two-thirds double entendre and one-third undis-guised seduction. I had a ball. For a change a woman was deliber-ately working on getting me heated up. Another difference from my usual situation with Janet, I wasn't getting all worked up for nothing. Karen played for keeps.

After dinner we walked the six blocks to the bar. The crisp coolness of the air was like an unwelcome astringent on my face. Christ, I thought, how in hell did I ever let myself get talked into this? I wanted to spend the evening with Helen and her friend like I wanted another hole in my head. God knows what Karen had told Helen about me and the relationship between us. Probably Karen had given Helen the idea that I was another one of her love-slaves who lived only for the occasional crumbs of friendship that Karen tossed my way.

Well, it was true, in part. I knew that Karen loved me in her own way. It was just too bad that her way wasn't mine. I was still in love with her, probably always would be in love with her. Love without hope is a funny thing. You can love someone else who feels the same way you do and still feel about someone as I felt about Karen and not have the latter detract from the former.

Our relationship would be different if I had any control over it. Karen was the one who called the shots though. What good did it do me to know that Karen cared for me when she refused to give up her other lovers? Maybe I would have been better off if I never saw her again. As things stood, I waited and suffered to be rewarded only occasionally … occasionally and wonderfully.

Karen was behaving in her typical manner this evening. She knew long in advance that I was coming to see her. Why hadn't she warned me that Helen would be there? She hadn't even told Helen to expect me.

And what if Helen went back to Oakwood and blabbed to Janet. I had tried so hard to make Janet think of me as strong and self-sufficient What would she think when she heard that Karen could manipulate me with a word? I'd never have a chance of getting near Janet if Helen told her I was having an affair with another woman.

I was in a lousy mood by the time we reached our destination. It was my first trip to a real gay bar and I should have been excited and curious but I only wanted to get it over with. Some fun, sitting around in a gin mill with the boss during my vacation. The hours ahead of me seemed infinite. It was going to be such a long time until I would be back in Karen's apartment and sipping happiness from her lips.

We had been silent during our walk. Now, as we walked down the steps and through the swinging door of the basement saloon, Karen leaned close to me and whispered, "I wish we hadn't promised them we'd meet them here tonight. I'd much rather be alone with you. Tell you what, we'll only stay a short while. Let's go home early. I want you, darling. Soon."

What a woman. She sure knew how to handle me. She had said exactly the right thing. My mood changed in a moment. Suddenly the world was a wonderful place and I was prepared to like everybody, even Helen Winsor.

The other couple was already seated at a table, waiting for us. Sandra, Helen's friend, was about my age. Our eyes met while we were being introduced and I could see by the expression in her eyes behind the thick glasses she wore that she was nervous and ill at ease. Karen whispered to me that Sandra was visiting a gay bar for the first time also. That gave us something in common which augmented my initial reaction to her. I had liked her immediately. She had such a down-to-earth no-nonsense quality about her that I knew right away she was a person with whom I could relax and be myself... whatever that is.

Helen and Karen were playing at being tour guides to Sandra and me. We gawked and exclaimed like the neophytes we were while the two old pros did their bit.

"You'll have to excuse the Hogarthian touch," Karen said. "Weekends and holidays all the exhibitionists in town come down here and vie for attention."

Sandra and I looked around the crowded room. At the women sitting at the bar, surrounded by slack-clad thin-hipped girls paying them court. At the tables where fresh-faced adolescents entwined fingers, where chic women in their late thirties and forties juggled the ice in their glasses while their desperate eyes roamed the room searching for young prey.

"Quite an assortment," Sandra said.

"Don't judge them too quickly, kids," Helen said. "I remember when I first came down here. I saw the whole thing as a ghastly ritual played by masks with no faces behind them. I'll admit my opinion of their behavior hasn't changed much but," Helen hesitated as she noticed Karen's mocking smile, "when you get to know them as individuals it becomes apparent that there is a quality of hopelessness about them that makes them need to act out this semi-ritualistic exorcism of their own personal devil...loneliness."

"Trite, but touching. And what about creatures like that one?" Karen queried, pointing toward a tall, masculine-looking woman who was leaning on the bar.

Something was going on that I didn't understand. Helen and Karen were waging a war of subtle digs at each other. Not as subtle as they thought because I was aware of it. I searched their faces for a clue but all I could make out was that they were both having a great time playing verbal tennis.

I directed my attention toward the woman at the bar. She had turned half-way around so that her profile was now visible. She looked familiar. That was impossible, I didn't know any women who would wear an outfit like hers. I tried to picture her with lipstick, longer hair and feminine apparel.

Sweet Jesus! It was Betty, the girl with whom I had shared Karen the previous summer! What had she done to herself? Only three months before she had been a cute kid. Now she looked like a homely man. Boy, some people didn't believe in wasting time. Betty had taken to homosexuality like the proverbial fish to water.

I was beginning to catch on. Karen was teasing Helen and me too. She didn't have to ask, "What about creatures like that one?" Karen would do something like this. Sandra's presence kept me from saying anything.

You know what about her as well as Helen and I do, Karen, I thought to myself. You had an affair with her a few months ago, remember? Or is three months too long for you to remember anyone, my sweet bitch of a lover?

Karen was testing us. She knew that seeing Betty dressed that way would upset Helen and me. And Karen was testing us to see if we could act objective and unconcerned when we hated the girl at the bar. Hated her for having possessed, however briefly, Karen. And now we would have to speak kindly of her while Karen laughed inwardly at our every word.

"Do you know that girl, Helen?" Sandra inquired innocently.

"I've met her," Helen answered curtly.

"Why does she dress that way?"

"What way?"

I relaxed back in my chair. I was off the hook. Sandra was making Helen carry the whole show by herself. Poor Sandra was obviously completely unaware of what was going on beneath the surface.

"Why," Sandra persisted, "you'd almost take her for a man if it wasn't for her hair. Even that's awfully short. Just long enough so she couldn't be a man."

"No, that's not all," Helen answered. "Look at her hands. They're too slender to be a man's and her fingernails are painted—not that that necessarily means anything down here. Look at her figure closely. Even that double-breasted suit she's wearing can't hide the bulge of her lips and thighs. On a man that jacket would taper down from the shoulders without that bulge across the front of the chest."

"But why does she want to dress that way?"

"That's an individual problem. Why anyone should want to change her sex is a big question. Everyone has their own peculiar reason for desiring it. What I don't understand is how anyone could be attracted to someone like that. She's neither fish nor fowl. Neither man nor woman."

I suppressed an impulse to applaud.

Karen accepted the dig goodnaturedly. Nevertheless, there was an insinuating coolness in her voice as she purred, "She's all woman ... when it counts."

Chalk one up for Karen. She won that round, hands,—or should I say, innuendoes—down.

Karen invited Betty to join our table. Betty and I went through the long-lost-brother routine even though we barely knew each other. I celebrated our little reunion party by buying a round of drinks.

Apparently, I had set a precedent. The four other women at our table took turns successively buying rounds of drinks. In a short while we were all zonked.

Betty's girlfriend finally came in to fetch her. From the weary smile on her face I gathered that she was accustomed to pouring Betty out of the place.

Betty had picked a lulu. I may be from the sticks but I can spot a stripper even with her clothes on when she looks like Betty's friend did. Fortunately, Betty was drunk enough to not notice the effect her lover's gutter vocabulary was having on us. Finally, the two of them sloshed out.

We were silent for a little while after Betty and her friend left. Everybody seemed to be absorbed in their own thoughts. I occupied myself with speculations about Betty. The poor kid was going down hill fast. Oh well, there was nothing I could do to stop her.

I looked around our table. Helen was leaning back against the upholstered wall behind her bench. The cigarette in her hand had a long, drooping ash. Her eyes were open but peculiarly vacant as seen through the mist of cigarette smoke that curled about her. She seemed to be thinking deeply about the ephemeral blue smoke before her but the slight twitch of the muscles of her left arm—the arm next to Karen—betrayed her. They were holding hands and I knew so well the amount of sensuality Karen could get into that small gesture, moving her palm ever so lightly against her companion's.

Karen wasn't looking at Helen. She didn't have to. She was saying everything she wanted to say by her touch.

Karen's gaze shifted from Sandra to me. Okay, so I had caught on an hour before that Sandra went for me. I wasn't for it. Sandra was a nice kid and I liked her but I wanted to keep it friendly. So I had ignored Sandra's attempts at flirtation, hoping that when she sobered up she wouldn't remember that I existed. I had played it down so that none of the others at our table would catch on. I didn't trust either of the older women to be tactful about the situation once they noticed it.

Karen had won again. It was obvious that she knew exactly what was going on. Worst of all, she knew that I was barely conscious of Sandra or anyone else, that she held my complete attention. Damn Karen for knowing it.

And damn her for playing with us this way. I didn't like what she was doing to Helen. Why couldn't she make up her mind? Was her affair with Helen a closed book or not? It was cruel of Karen to prolong any agonies of withdrawal of love which Helen might be suffering.

"Want to go home, Sandra?" Helen asked.

"No. Not yet. Let's stay a little while longer."

Helen looked worried and angry. Couldn't blame her, she was responsible for Sandra's ever being in the bar. Sandra was exhibiting a growing taste for morbidity—one of the first steps toward total immersion in homosexual life.

Karen laughed deep in her throat. "Anxious, Helen? The evening's young and you're showing your age. The kids are having fun."

"What kids? You, you mean. Why don't you let them speak for themselves?"

Karen's eyebrows twitched in a quickly-erased frown. "Don't get nasty, honey. I was just riding you a little bit." She smiled. "I can understand your being anxious to be alone with Sandra. She's lovely, simply lovely."

Karen had done it again. She had had the last word. The one that can't be contradicted because it was flattering—to Sandra and to Helen. And it was rude, too. Presumptuously rude.

Much later Karen said, "Let's go. I'm getting sick of this place."

"We were all comfortably blurred by then so that our separate identities had become one with the alcohol-powered treadmill about us.

"Yes, I guess it is getting late," Sandra glanced at her watch. "My God, it's 3:30!"

"Correct." Karen signalled to the waiter to bring the check. "And it'll be four o'clock before we get you two home and four-thirty by the time Paula and I hit the sack."

"I've got an idea," Helen said. "Sandra has plenty of room in her apartment. What about all of us staying there tonight. That way you won't have to drive all the way back downtown."

Karen smiled. "You're too anxious, my love."

Helen's face turned white, as if she had been struck. "I...I didn't mean it that way,"

"Of course you did," Karen laughed. "Don't let it bother you, I think it was a charming suggestion. I'll take a raincheck on it. C'mon, everybody. Let's go."

CHAPTER FIVE

I tripped over a pile of books entering the apartment.

"Don't you ever clean this place up?"

"It's clean. A little untidy, I'll admit, but you could eat off the floor."

"At the moment, I'd rather lie on it. I'm beat."

"Delightful image. Care to join me?" Karen dropped her coat on the rug and crumpled herself down upon it, her pose languid and waiting.

So much blondeness. White and gold against a background of red.

I walked away, my jaw set. Angrily, I shoved the hanger bearing my coat into the closet. Several minutes were spent digging in my pocketbook for cigarettes suddenly turned elusive.

I returned to the living room, my head bent over a flaming match.

Karen was still lying on the floor. Her eyes closed, fingers loosened, she looked asleep. I knew she wasn't. I stood above her not knowing what to do next.

"Say something."

Karen opened her eyes and smiled languidly.

"What would you like me to say?" She twisted her body, drawing her skirt up above her knees. "I'll say anything you'd like. This is the first time in ages we've been alone together so will 'hello' do for a start?"

I grinned. "Appropriate but inadequate."

"May I add that I've missed you."

"You have an odd way of showing it. I saw you holding hands with Helen, you know. Are you sure you wouldn't rather have her here?"

"Uh-uh, don't get morbid. It's up to you to blind me to Helen's charms. Come, offer me something which will blind me to all others."

"You're the hostess, Karen. You're supposed to be giving me tokens of your hospitality. Well, what am I going to get?"

"Everything you deserve, darling. Everything you deserve."

The next morning, lying in bed listening to the comfortable sound of Karen's relaxed breathing, I debated with myself whether or not to regret the previous night. Would I come to feel as I had so often in the past that I had lived one day too long? The previous night had been so beautiful, so complete in itself. Immersed in love, past hurts had disappeared, future sorrows rendered improbable.

Was it worth it? To love a human being as one loves beauty? Fully, without hope. It was impossible, of course, to suspend possessiveness. But for the moment, holding Karen in my arms, I had possessed her.

Karen pulled the strings, there was no denying that. She didn't even attempt to hide the pleasure she derived from exercising her power. Control slipped away from her in bed, however. Lust was Karen's undoing.

I adored Karen at those moments when I could call forth unreasoning passion in her. And then the utter dependence of the act of love itself. In my hands, in my lips lay the capacity to bring Karen to the point—and then to leave her undone, possessed.

I turned on my side and fed my eyes on Karen's lush blondeness. With my hand I brushed a lock of hair from her forehead.

Karen opened her eyes and smiled sleepily. "Morning?"

"No. You."

"Love me?"

"Do I have a choice?"

"No." Karen extended her arms toward me. "You do love me?"

"So very much."

Karen smiled slightly. "Come here."

We embraced and touched faces and mouths as children do—with freshness and sweetness.

CHAPTER SIX

P reparations for the Christmas play were begun immediately
  after Thanksgiving vacation. The Christmas Play Committee
was composed of six teachers. Harriet Moore served, as she had
for fifteen years, as committee chairman. She was the only established teacher in the school who didn't spend the time from summer recess until fall inventing reasons why they couldn't possibly
find the time to be a member of the committee. Indeed, Harriet
Moore looked forward to assuming her duties. Hers was the task
of stimulating enthusiasm where there had been apathy, coop-
eration where there had been thinly disguised rebellion. Among
the numerous methods by which this might be accomplished,
Harriet Moore chose bullying.

Janet and I had received notice of our appointment to the
Christmas Play Committee in early October. Since neither of us
had ever been even remotely associated with dramatics before it was
inevitable that we be designated joint directors and heads of casting.

The play that year was to be *Amahl and the Night Visitors.*
This ambitious project was the choice of Harriet Moore who,
flushed with the accolades of the P.T.A. for her previous pre-
sentations, was anxious to prove her boundless abilities with a
demanding musical work. Miss Moore's frustrated ambition to
be a concert pianist and her inevitable selection as accompanist
played no small role in her decision to foist *Amahl and the Night
Visitors* onto the doting members of the P.T.A.

Auditions were completed early in December and the play
was due to go into rehearsal in two days when Janet and I received

memorandums advising us of a special committee meeting to be held during our lunch break that day.

The Teachers' Lounge was empty when we entered, the rest of the faculty all being in the cafeteria at the time. Janet collapsed onto a couch and lit a cigarette.

I stood at the window looking out at the schoolyard. The tensions and fatigue of the morning slipped away from me as I stood there. It had been a tough day. The proud outlines of the trees shaking their sere leaves loose soothed me. Life is a process not only of growth but of shedding of characteristics no longer appropriate, they seemed to be saying to me. Nothing is right if it doesn't suit the occasion. Strength lies in adaptability.

Harriet Moore let the door bang shut behind her in her customary manner. She was always rushing about, dropping things, pushing things out of her way, running distracted fingers through her touseled hair as if she had more important matters to deal with than these trivia. She sat down on a straight chair opposite Janet and pulled a typewritten sheet from her briefcase.

I joined Janet on the couch and regarded Harriet with amusement. We had gotten along without clashes so far but we had been warned by other teachers of the deadly seriousness with which Harriet regarded even the smallest detail of the play's presentation.

Janet and I had decided that there weren't going to be any emotional crises this year. We would agree to everything within reason that Harriet wanted. It wouldn't be worth opposing her since Harriet usually got her way in the end anyway.

Harriet extended the typewritten sheets toward us.

"I found these in my mailbox this morning. I believe these are your final casting decisions."

"Yes," Janet replied. "We had elimination auditions yesterday after school. I got the list to you as soon as I could."

Taking the sheets back, Harriet Moore folded them in her lap and twisted in her chair to look out the window for a long moment. When she looked back at us she had composed her face into what she obviously thought was an expression of maternal understanding.

"I see you've chosen Stanley DeCantro to play Amahl."

"Oh yes." Janet leaned forward, a light of enthusiasm in her eyes. "He's perfect for the part. He's got such a sweet voice and even though he is a fifth grader, he's small for his age and would look right for the part of Amahl. After all, we can't have the child being taller than his mother or the three wise men. Do you know him?"

"Yes, he was in my class last year. He's very cooperative and I understand that he's a member of the choir at Our Lady of Sorrows Church. But, Janet and Paula, I'm afraid he won't do for the part."

"But why? Stanley sings beautifully and if he's been singing in a choir, he'll have stage presence. It's a very demanding role for a child and we need someone who can practically carry the show alone."

"You said it, Jan." I smiled ruefully. "God knows we'll have to make enthusiasm substitute for talent with most of the cast. We had to choose between kids who sounded as if they were drowning whenever they hit a high note and those who only seemed to have been confronted with an underfed tiger. The latter group got the parts."

Harriet's smile was brief and quickly replaced by an earnest pursing of her lips.

"Children, I've been teaching a lot longer than you have. There are many things to consider in an undertaking like ours. Things that don't have to do with talent.

"I was standing at the back of the auditorium yesterday. I heard Stanley sing and I agree that he has an exceptional voice. But he simply cannot be Amahl. I'm not sure that he should be in the play at all. However, in view of his abilities, I suggest that we let him play one of the minor roles."

"But why?" Janet asked.

"Oakwood is a small town but a wealthy one," Harriet said, assuming her best lectern manner. "Most of the people living here own the same land on which their families have been growing tobacco for generations. They're tightly knit. The Grange meetings have more power in deciding municipal policy than the mayor. The farmers have not only money but also the tradition of land ownership to back them up. They're hostile to newcomers and with good reason. During the war the factories put up housing for itinerant workers on land that could have been used for cultivation. You don't see the people who sold them that land at Grange meetings. Most of them took the money that they had made from the sale of the land and moved away. Whether they wanted to go or whether they were forced to move by the group pressure doesn't matter.

"Most of the factory workers also moved away after the war. A few of them stayed to work in the tobacco fields or to set up small shops. They have been treated decently. However, they're not welcome beyond certain limits. Their ways are different. They don't appreciate the things that are important to people whose families have been a part of this community for generations.

"Stanley DeCantro's father was a tool-maker during the war. Now he runs a vegetable stand out on the highway. The DeCantros are decent, hardworking people. They keep to themselves and so are respected. However, one could hardly call the DeCantros 'gentry'."

"I don't care if they're horse thieves!" Janet's face was flushed with anger. "Stanley DeCantro is only a child. He has as much right to get up on that stage and show off or make an ass of himself as any other child in this school!"

Harriet Moore's smile was as sweet and sticky as twopenny candy. "Profanity won't be necessary, dear. I know how you feel. Nevertheless, we must face reality. There are no DeCantros or anyone else with a name like that on the schoolboard. The

Adams, Harrisons and Franklins have controlled this town and educational system in it ever since Oakwood got its first one-room school. They're not going to like it if their children aren't given the principal roles in our play. The Christmas play is very important to the school. All the local people come to see it. We've always had the children of the best families in our plays. Parents enjoy seeing their children on stage. If the parents are pleased they leave us alone and we can run the school in our own way. If they didn't like the Christmas play, I shudder to think of what Miss Winsor would have to face at the January meeting of the Board of Education.

"Now, girls, don't you think that Don Franklin would make and adorable Amahl? The Franklins and Harrisons are neighbors out on the South Road. Since you have Dulcie Harrison playing Amahl's mother, I think it would be very sweet if Don Franklin could be Amahl."

"That sniveling brat! I wouldn't have him play a stage prop. He's the most ill-mannered child I've ever met. He was so sure that he'd be Amahl that he had to be forced to attend auditions. No, Miss Moore, I will not have Don Franklin in the play. Now, if you'll excuse us, we haven't had any lunch yet. Come on, Jan." I rose from the couch and headed toward the door.

"Sit down!" Harriet Moore's command was loud and sharp as the report of a rifle in the small room.

We went back to the couch, awed by the authority in Miss Moore's voice.

"Miss Harman and Miss Coxe, you two have got a lot to learn. I've dealt with people like you two before. You come out of Teachers College full of ideas and think you can change the world. You can't. You're going to have to learn that sometime and I think this is as good a time as any.

"Since both of you feel so strongly about Don Franklin, there's no use forcing you to put him in the play. I'm well aware of what a director can do to make a performer look foolish. Making a fool out of Don Franklin would be worse than not having him in the play at all. I'll concede on that one point.

"However, I insist that we have a child of one of the prominent local families play the part of Amahl. I don't care who it is so long as his name means something in Oakwood!"

Anger was nearly choking me, threatening to silence the words I felt I must say. "Stanley DeCantro is going to play that part or I'm going to resign as director. He's been promised the part and I'm not going to be responsible for his misery when he finds that it has been taken away from him."

"That goes double for me," Janet said. "Stanley's all excited about the play. It's the first time he has ever been given any recognition. His family is awfully proud of him. His mother telephoned me last night to tell me how happy she is. I refused to be a party to humiliating Stanley or any member of his family. Please accept my resignation from the Christmas Play Committee."

"You can't resign, either of you!" Harriet Moore's belligerent expression had given way to one of fear. "How would it look? People would ask questions. There might be talk. I had hoped that you would understand my position as being for the good of the school. Since you refuse to listen to reason, I'm not going to argue further now. I've called a committee meeting for this afternoon after school. I had hoped that we could discuss our publicity campaign at the meeting. However, because you two insist on being so stubborn, we'll have to waste time putting the matter up to a vote of the committee. I trust you'll abide by their decision?"

"No, we won't!" Janet said. "You force me to be frank, Miss Moore. No one on that committee gives a damn about the play except you. They're only interested in getting it over with the least possible expenditure of time and energy. If it comes to opposing you and possibly getting you to snoop into the way they've been handling their duties, I think the majority of them would rather vote in your favor than face the consequences. We insist on a more impartial judge."

"You mean Miss Winsor?" Harriet Moore's eyes glinted with malice. "Don't think that I don't know how much influence you have with her, Miss Coxe. But I'll bring her in on this if you insist. She's been Principal of this school long enough to respect my opinion. Helen Winsor and I went to college together. I think that may carry as much weight as your pretty face."

Confusion deprived me of words. What was Harriet hinting at? How much did she know? Were all the teachers aware of Helen's attraction to Janet? If that was true, than they probably knew about me too. Did they think that Janet and I were living together as lovers.

The bell sounded, signalling the end of lunch. As we walked toward our classrooms, Harriet said, "Let's get this matter settled as soon as possible. We can have a meeting in the Principal's office tomorrow before school. I'll notify Helen and if it's all right with her, I'll let you know before three this afternoon."

The next morning Janet and I left for school an hour earlier than usual. We thought we'd be the first ones there but as soon as we entered the building we heard Harriet Moore's high-pitched voice coming from the Principal's office. We could hear her clearly all the way out in the corridor.

A murmured, "Come in," answered Janet's knock. She pushed open the door to the Principal's office.

Helen Winsor was sitting behind her desk. Her head was resting on the palm of one hand and she held a fizzing glass of Alka Seltzer in the other. Her usually immaculate appearance had given way that morning to the effect of what was obviously a monumental hangover. Black hollows encircled her eyes. Helen's trim grey gabardine suit looked as if she had slept in it. Wispy bits of white hair were escaping from the bun she wore low on her neck. Her usually fresh-looking healthy complexion was the blotchy grey color of the paste that kindergarten children make from flour and water.

"Good morning." Helen fairly groaned the words out. "Sit down, gently, please. Let's see if we can discuss this whole matter quietly. Harriet here has been bellowing about some trouble with the Christmas play. Tell me your side of it. And speak softly or I'll murder the three of you."

Helen leaned back in her swivel chair and winced as the spring creaked.

"What happened to you?" Janet asked, looking shocked and concerned.

I was almost as shocked as Janet. I had never before seen Helen looking that way. She was forty-five and usually looked thirty except for her white hair. That morning she looked sixty at least.

"A friend of mine from New York visited me last night. It got to be too late for her to drive back so she decided to stay up all night and drive back in the morning. She left an hour ago. I've been here in my office since then trying to clear up some work so that I could leave early today. I'm so tired I don't think I could last the whole day."

I searched Helen's face for some hint of who her "friend from New York" was. It could have been Sandra Munson. I dismissed that possibility. Sandra wasn't the type to make a two hundred mile trip overnight. No, it couldn't be Sandra, she didn't own a car. What about Karen? Had Karen collected on that "raincheck" last night? Damn it, why did Harriet and Janet have to be there. I could have asked Helen if it was Karen if those two hadn't been with us.

If it had been Karen, maybe I was better off not knowing. If she had been right there in Oakwood for the night and hadn't even bothered telephoning me to say hello, I was probably better off not knowing about it. After all, it needn't have been Karen. Helen knew lots of people from New York. It could have been anyone.

Just as I was beginning to convince myself that there was no reason for jealousy, that Helen's friend could be just an old school chum or someone she had picked up in a gay bar on one of her frequent visits to New York, Helen looked at me. There was an expression of suppressed triumph in Helen's eyes. That was as good as spelling it out in neon lights. So it had been Karen who had driven two hundred miles to spend one night with Helen. The old girl must be hell on wheels in bed to make it worth a trip like that and staying up all night.

Janet was speaking. "Since you don't feel well, maybe we ought to let this go until tomorrow or Monday."

Harriet Moore turned swiftly around from where she had been standing looking out the window and acknowledged our presence for the first time.

"We will not let this go another minute longer," she said through clenched teeth. "By Monday the whole town will know that you're giving the part to Stanley DeCantro."

"Who in hell is Stanley DeCantro?" Helen asked.

Harriet sniffed. "He's a fifth grader in Frank Yellen's class. His father runs a vegetable stand out on the highway. Really, Helen, I should think that you'd know him. He's been in this school for five years. If you'd take more interest in your work and less in carousing around all night, you'd know who we were talking about."

"I do know who you mean now." Helen sounded too worn out for anger. "I just forgot who he was for a moment. After all, I don't have too much to do with individual children unless they're brought in here because of behavior problems. And may I suggest that we hold the impeachment proceedings some other time? Let's get back to that earth-shaking problem that can't be put off until Monday."

"Paula and I chose Stanley DeCantro for the part of Amahl in the Christmas play because we felt that he was the best suited for the part," Janet began, "and Miss Moore feels that we should have chosen someone who was more representative of the local powers that be. Briefly, we argued about it and couldn't reach an agreement. Paula and I offered to resign. Miss Moore wouldn't let us because she said it would provoke a scandal."

"I will not have the whole town discussing the internal affairs of the school." Harriet bent close over Helen's desk to emphasize her point. Catching the smell of stale Scotch on Helen's breath, Harriet turned away and resumed her pacing. "I think this problem can be settled right here. There's no reason for dragging outsiders in on it."

"Then why are you yelling loud enough to be heard all over the building? Harriet, if you don't lower your voice I'm going to call off this whole discussion. Now, Janet, why do you want Stanley for the part?"

"Because he has the most talent. He can sing. He has stage presence. He's good-looking and he's a sweet charming child who's a joy to work with." Janet paused and glared at Harriet Moore's back. "She wants us to give the part to Don Franklin. I'm sure you know who he is. He's been sent to your office on every charge from chewing gum in class to writing dirty words on the lavatory walls. Besides, he can't sing."

"I fully agree with Janet that Don Franklin has no business representing the school," Helen smiled ironically, "let alone the spirit of Christmas. What made you want him, Harriet?"

"Oh, it wasn't him that I wanted necessarily." Harriet's manner was almost pleading. "I just thought it would be best for public relations to have the son of one of the more prominent families play the leading role. I don't care who she chooses … just so long as it isn't the DeCantro boy or someone else of his sort"

"A policy you've followed in all the years that you've been chairman of the Christmas Play Committee. Fortunately for you, no one's ever questioned your dictatorship before." But, Helen's anger was getting the better of her fatigue. "This time it's your own fault. Harriet, you should never have chosen *Amahl and the Night Visitors* for performance by a bunch of untrained elementary school kids. This is nothing but a vehicle for you to show off your prowess as a pianist. That fact will be apparent to the audience two minutes after the curtain goes up."

"However, since the play has already been chosen and it's too late to do anything about it now, we'll have to deal with the facts at hand. How good is this DeCantro boy?"

"Oh, he's really excellent for the part. He can sing and act and..."

"I know how you feel about him, Janet," Helen broke in. "For the moment, I'm interested in hearing Harriet's opinion."

"Well, I've only seen him auditioning, of course. He does sing nicely and he didn't seem flustered out on the stage. But then many children are at their best only in front of a real audience."

"You agree then, Harriet, that Stanley DeCantro is a good performer?"

"Yes. But..."

Helen's lips quivered in the beginning of a smile. "And do you honestly think that there is any other child in this school who could handle the role as well as he?"

"No but," Harriet stopped her pacing and glared at Janet and me as she realized the direction in which Helen's questioning was going, "I think the question to be decided here is whether the Christmas play is to be regarded as one would a professional work. In that case, ability and talent would naturally be considered in the assigning of roles. We are not, however, attempting to set up a stock company in Oakwood. I think we all agree that the Christmas Play is given before an adult audience as a gesture toward promoting better public relations in the community for the school. With that in mind, I fail to see how Stanley DeCantro could possibly be any help in inducing the Board of Education to enlarge our cafeteria."

"Your loyalty and interest in the school are commendable, Harriet," Helen replied sarcastically. "However, you are not facing certain facts. Times have changed. These days the DeCantros and the other newer residents of Oakwood like them have a great deal of political influence. The old tobaccogrowing families are in the statistical minority now. It won't be long before the newer residents will be sufficiently organized to elect their own town officials. I, for one, am looking forward to that day. I've always thought that Oakwood's political setup smacked of feudalism.

"Be that as it may," Helen leaned forward in her chair, "that's not the issue here. You've asked for my opinion so I'll give it to you. I don't believe that Stanley should get the role because he represents the newcomers any more than that Don Franklin should just because his great-great-great-grandfather came to Oakwoods in order to escape a prison sentence in England. My opinion, for what it's worth, is that Stanley DeCantro is the obvious choice for the part of Amahl because he has the most ability."

"You don't know what you're saying!" Harriet's voice shook with emotion. "Why, you yourself come from one of the finest families in this state. Your mother was president of the Hartford chapter of the D.A.R. Are you forgetting that you're a Windsor, Helen?"

"Sometimes I'd like to. Let me set you straight on a few matters. I haven't been to a D.A.R, meeting since I was old enough to know what it was all about. Furthermore, I'm insulted that our long years of friendship have left you with nothing better to say about me than that my ancestors once did something mildly commendable."

Helen's voice became softer, more kindly. "Harriet, I think it's about time you examined your thinking. If you want to be the pawn of the Adams, Harrisons, and Franklin's, that's one thing. And if you want to be a worthwhile teacher, that's another. Then your primary responsibility is to your students and not their parents.

"You asked me for my opinion and now you have it. Ordinarily, I'd just give you my views on the matter and let the three of you work out a solution. Not in this case, however. I will not permit the De Cantro boy to suffer any humiliation because of my pusillanimity. As Principal of this school I demand that Stanley be given the part. Now, clear out of here, all of you, so that I can get some work done."

Janet and I started for the door. Harriet remained standing where she was. She apparently had no intention of leaving so I just shut the door and left her there.

Opposite to the Principal's office were the teachers' mailboxes. We stopped to check ours. There was a letter from the Oakwood Superintendent of Schools waiting for each of us. There were still a few minutes left before classes began so Janet and I stood in the corridor reading our letters.

The Superintendent's letter was just a routine mimeographed sheet welcoming the new teachers and outlining umpty-nine extra-curricular duties the Superintendent felt he had to remind his little slaves about. There was nothing in the letter except the usual garbage but we read it through carefully. You never could tell in advance whether or not the Superintendent had thought up some new nonsense. The Superintendent had a reputation for personally making sure every teacher sweated for her crummy thirty-six hundred per annum.

We were reading the letters when I became aware of the sounds of a heated argument coming from Helen's office. I looked up from the letter and saw that Janet was also listening. Standing so close, we could hear every word being said in the Principal's office.

"That was a pretty little speech you gave, Helen."

We could hear the honey-coated sarcasm in Harriet's voice as clearly as if we had been right in the room with her.

"You were so vehement, dear," Harriet went on. "In all the years I've known you I've never heard such an impassioned diatribe. Be honest with me, dear. Were you really all that outraged? Weren't you really playing crusader for Janet's benefit? Championing Janet's cause against that of an older colleague and long-time friend was really a bit much, don't you think? I mean, if you wanted to play the gallant for Janet, I do think it would have been wiser to choose a less important situation."

"Godammit, Harriet, I took Janet's side only because she was in the right! I would have been truly showing prejudice if I had agreed with you. I think you're wrong in this matter and I gave you plenty of reasons why I think so." Helen gave a moan of frustration. "What's the use of arguing with you? I should have realized that nothing I said would make the slightest impression on you. You never consider moral and ethical principles. Everything you do is emotionally motivated, Harriet. Where you make your mistake is in presuming that everyone else does the same. It's completely beyond you to imagine that anyone could possibly want to do anything just because their conscience tells them to do it."

"Helen dear, after all these years, I'm surprised that you can't be more honest with me. There's no need to hide anything. You know that I know everything about your—uh—unusual interest. This is hardly the first time you've become infatuated with one of the new teachers. We've always been able to discuss your 'attachments' before. I don't understand why you feel it neccesary to be circumspect this time. It's perfectly obvious to me that you're attracted to Janet. It doesn't make any difference to me, you know I've always tried to be understanding about your abnormality, Helen. Your interest in Janet needn't make any difference in our friendship. Although I must admit that if I were you or if I desired members of my own sex as you do—and I thank God that I don't—I would choose the Harman girl. She's much prettier, don't you agree?"

"There have been moments in the past when I've wondered why I continued to be your friend," Helen replied. "There have even been times when I felt a strong desire to use violence to stop you from spewing out your ugly, warped thoughts. This is one of those times, Harriet. I won't deny that what you say about my affection for Janet is true. You know me too well. I couldn't hide something like that from you. What I do object to is your rotten insinuation that I decided the issue of the Christmas Play in Janet's favor because I have more affection for her than I do for you.

"Harriet, I'm warning you, if you ever so much as hint to Janet that I displayed favoritism, I'll ... I don't know what I'd do. Let her alone, Harriet. I don't want her contaminated by you. She's young and unafraid and beautiful now. I want her to stay that way."

"For you, Helen?"

"Yes, for me, since you must know!" Helen shouted. "Now get the hell out of here before I do something we'd both regret!"

I had been standing still, paralyzed by shock and curiosity. Now I grabbed Janet's arm and pulled her with me down the corridor.

"Let's get going. If Harriet sees us standing by the mailbox, she'll know we heard them."

"Paula, I don't understand. What were they ... "

"Never mind that for now," I said "We've got to get to our classrooms."

CHAPTER SEVEN

Like it or not, there was no denying that I was going to have a difficult situation on my hands. Harriet and Helen had dropped a nice little time bomb into my lap. Sooner or later Janet was sure to question me about the conversation we had over heard. Maybe I'd be able to lie myself out of any knowledge about the whole topic and maybe I wouldn't. Janet was a smart little cookie. It would take a clear mind and lots of determination to fool her about anything. Those two qualities are profoundly lacking in me. Particularly in a situation like this one where I couldn't make up my mind which attitude would be the best to assume. Whatever I finally decided, I knew for sure that Janet wouldn't let me just forget about the matter. As I've said, sooner or later I'd have to discuss it with her. I preferred to make it later.

Somehow or other I managed to do my job that day. My panic wasn't bad during the day because I was safe in the classroom.

When school was over at three o'clock, Janet trapped me in the Teachers' Lounge. She took me aside and asked me if I would come home with her right away. She said she wanted to talk to me about something.

"Something" indeed! I knew all too well what was on her mind. I wasn't ready to cope with it yet so I told her that I had to do some research in the library and wouldn't get home until dinnertime. That gave me a three-hour reprieve. Not much but at that point I would have welcomed a five minute postponement.

I went to the library allright. Big fat lot of good that did me. I just sat in a chair with my head in my hands trying to figure out what to say. Damn that Helen Winsor. Why couldn't she keep her flabby lesbian mouth shut.

I left the library still not knowing what to do. On the way home, however, I cooked up a good story to tell Janet. I reviewed it carefully in my mind, checking it for loopholes. It was perfect. Janet would never suspect that I was lying. She would think that I was as bewildered by Harriet and Helen's conversation as she was. With that story I came across like the most heterosexual, the normallest.

I walked into the house completely confident, took one look at Janet looking indescribably beautiful and desirable, and promptly forgot every word of my carefully thought-out deception. There was nothing I could do, I'd have to play it by ear.

Janet had our dinner all ready. She set it out on the table and called to me to join her before the stew got cold.

I was so nervous I could hardly eat. Janet pretended not to notice. I knew that she had sensed my tension. I could tell by the frantic efforts she made to put me at my ease. After a while her efforts paid off. I began laughing at her jokes and before long the two of us were clowning it up all over the kitchen.

I began to think that possibly I wouldn't have to answer any questions. Janet didn't seem to want to press anything. She had probably forgotten all about the morning's happenings.

It was my turn to wash the dishes. We worked it that way. When one of us cooked dinner the other washed the dishes. Often, Janet would stay in the kitchen talking to me while I washed up. That night she stayed at her desk correcting papers.

I took that to be another good sign. I was so sure that I wouldn't have to face a crisis that night that I actually enjoyed washing the dishes ... which, for me, is like enjoying batting your head against a brick wall.

I finished the dishes and walked out to the living room. Janet looked up from her work.

"Hi," she said. "I've been waiting for you to get through so I'd have company while I goof off. I'm going to make myself another cup of coffee. Want some?"

"Yes, make a cup for me, please." Of hemlock? I sat down on the couch and relaxed in the blissful ignorance of abysmal stupidity.

Janet came back with the coffee. She handed me my cup then sat herself down on the opposite end of the couch.

She was invitingly near me. Only about two feet separated us. Two feet of soft couch that could be put to such delicious use. Good little girls have visions of sugar plums dancing in their heads. Not me, my fantasies were of a distinctly different nature.

"Talk to me."

Janet startled me out of my reveries.

"What about?"

A deep frown furrowed Janet's forehead. "I've been thinking about this morning. I don't understand it. Not all of it, anyway. Paula, help me. I feel so confused and naive. Tell me what's going on."

I was deep in the grand-daddy of all anxiety attacks. My mind had become a whirling mass of disconnected phrases. As hard as I tried, I couldn't think of how to answer her.

"Please, Paula. I feel like the guest of honor at a banquet who doesn't know why he's being toasted."

Then she made everything worse by reaching over and taking my hand.

"You're trembling. Why, Paula? Are you afraid that you might shock me? Don't worry. I'm not as innocent as you think I am. I know how Helen feels about me. Or at least, how Harriet thinks Helen feels about me."

"You tell me then," I managed to croak.

"Okay, if you prefer it that way. Only I wish you would relax. You shouldn't be this way. Nothing could change the way I feel about you. Don't you know that I love you, Paula?"

I glanced at her quickly.

"You're the best friend I've ever had," Janet added.

I should have known that that was what she meant. I was a fool to have thought, even for a second, that Janet loved me as I loved her.

"Please, honey, stop looking like you wished you were dead. I've wanted to talk to you about this before now but I was always afraid you'd laugh at me if I did."

"I won't laugh, Janet." I didn't add that I might have a heart attack though.

"Okay," Janet began. "For one thing, I can tell you that I've read a lot of books. Also, I'm not blind, deaf or outstandingly stupid. I've experienced a lot of different things and heard about a lot of others."

Why couldn't she get on with it. I could do without the preamble.

Janet sighed deeply before continuing.

"Look, I'm going to speak as plainly as I can. Helen Winsor is homosexual. We both know that. Harriet Moore thinks that Helen is attracted to me. I'm not too sure that's true. I know Helen said she was but I think she was trying to throw Harriet off the scent. If anything, I suspect that she might be interested in you. However, I'm not sure that that's true either."

I began to relax a little. Janet was carrying the ball beautifully all by herself.

"I think you're wrong," I said. "I don't think Helen's attracted to me at all. I have reason to believe she's in love with someone else. Someone she knew long before she met either of us."

"Your friend Karen?"

The panic came back full force. It was so bad that I automatically jerked away, pulling my hand out of Janet's.

"They don't even know each other."

Janet laughed richly. "You're a terrible liar, Paula. Either that or you've lost your memory. Don't you remember telling me all about your trip to New York? You told me about running into Helen at Karen's apartment. You also told me about going to a gay bar with the two of them and some other girl. You said that you all went there as tourists and found it interesting though depressing."

Dear Lord, why did I have to be born with a silver foot in my mouth? I didn't have to tell Janet about the gay bar. I could have told her anything and she wouldn't have known the difference. Instead, I had to go and tell her about the one incriminating thing I had done that whole week. Heaven only knows why I hadn't also told her about going to bed with Karen too. It was so unlike me to have had the sense not to describe every detail. I probably would have finished off that little story by telling Janet that I did it as an experiment, or for laughs, or because it was the chic thing to do this season. And I probably would have expected Janet to swallow my explanation wholesale.

"Tell me the truth, Paula. Helen and Karen aren't just friends, are they? Their relationship is unnatural, isn't it?"

" 'Unnatural!' Don't ever use that word again! I won't have you talk about Karen this way! You don't even know her. What right have you to accuse her of something like this! I don't care what you think Helen is, but I won't have you say that Karen and she are anything more than friends."

I knew I was lying even as I said the words. I couldn't help myself. I was nearly suffocating with anger. I felt as though Janet were taking Karen away from me. As though she was giving her to Helen.

"Are you in love with Karen?"

"No."

"Don't lie to me, Paula."

"I'm not lying to you. Why are you asking me all these questions?"

"I think I have a right to know."

Something snapped inside me. I didn't care what I said. I was so furious I wanted to hit Janet.

"Why you sanctimonious fool … "

"You don't understand," Janet interrupted. "I didn't mean it that way."

"Don't try to deny it. I know very well what you meant. And you know what I'm going to do? I'm going to answer your snooping questions. I'm going to tell you about myself. I want you to know me for what I really am. Don't worry, though. My condition isn't contagious."

I took a deep breath before continuing. "I've told you the truth. I don't love Karen. Not in the way you meant. Not anymore. But I did love her once. Fully and completely, the way a man would love a woman. She meant everything to me."

I stopped and thought back to that far away time that was too exquisite ever to forget. The long ago time when I had been happy. Slowly, as if I were talking to myself, I told Janet about meeting Karen at the camp. About the friendship that had started the day I tripped coming back from the shower and Karen had looked out her door just as the towel had dropped off me. And I told her about the way our friendship had grown to be something else. And about the bright bubble of happiness that had burst when I had learned that Karen would never be completely mine.

I had kept my eyes shut, watching with the eye of memory tableaus of infinite sweetness and infinite pain. When I reached the end of my narrative, I opened my eyes and looked at Janet.

She was still sitting at the opposite end of the couch. Her mouth was open slightly. Her whole posture conveyed rigid attention. She looked as if she were afraid to move. As if she feared any movement on her part might make me stop reciting my incredible history.

Once again panic took hold of me. What was I doing? Why was I telling Janet all this? The need to continue was strong in me. I had told no one about the summer and the amazing revelations that had come to me then. But why unburden myself to Janet? Why not someone else? Why did I want her to know about the most meaningful thing in my whole life? How could she understand what I was telling her? Suppose she despised me for being what I was?

"I know what you're thinking," I said scornfully. "You're wondering how juicy this is going to turn out to be. Well, just because I'm such a good little roommate, I'm going to tell you everything."

My hands were trembling, my voice becoming shrill with rising hysteria. "I slept with Karen. Do you hear me, Janet? I slept with her, made love to her, had sex with her, call it what you want."

Still Janet did not move.

"All right, my fine New England buddy, why don't you say it?" I tried to keep my voice and eyes hard but there was a softening about my entire body which betrayed how near to tears I was. "Why don't you say that if you had known about this you never would have taken an apartment with me? Don't you understand what I'm telling you? I'm a lesbian!"

I looked at Janet's still expressionless face for a long moment and then I slumped forward and began to cry helplessly.

Janet came rushing over to the other side of the couch and put her arms around me, pulling me to my feet.

Gently, she urged me toward the bedroom. Through my sobs I could hear her trying to soothe me. She was telling me that this was no time for rights and wrongs. That she was my friend. Janet was saying that although she didn't understand all that I had been telling her, she knew that I had been hurt deeply and that as my friend she wanted to do what she could to lessen the pain.

Also, Janet said, without knowing why, she felt as if this hurt had been hers also and that in consoling me she was somehow consoling herself.

We were in the bedroom. Gently, she urged me down on the bed.

I started to loosen my hold around Janet's shoulder and then tightened it again, pulling Janet down with me.

"Don't go away. Not now. Not yet. Stay with me, please. You're so beautiful, Janet. Like something which is good but untouchable. I want to touch you, Janet, please. Lovely, lovely Janet. I was young before this summer too. I'm old now, Janet. Make me young again."

My speech was broken and half-hysterical, punctuated by sobs that shivered through my body and pressed it closer and closer to Janet's. She too was crying, softly.

I raised my hand and began brushing the tears off Janet's face. One droplet hung at the corner of her eye. I bent down to kiss it away. And then another that rolled back toward the fragrant black hair above Janet's ear. And I kissed the path of that tear too. And then Janet's ear lying small and secretive in the dimnight mass of her hair. And then her throat, so warm, so smooth, so defenceless.

Janet was crooning something softly under her breath. It sounded like a lullaby that had been filtered through a New Orleans jazz mill.

My lips moved slowly over Janet's hot skin until they came to rest in a little place below her chin where my ear was brushed by the sweet breath of Janet's song.

We fell asleep in that position.

I woke up first. For a moment I looked at Janet sleeping next to me and wondered what she was doing there. As I recalled the events of the previous evening a feeling of joyous wonder came over me. Janet loved me. I knew that now.

I even had reason to hope that some day Janet would love me in the way in which I loved her. That she would surrender herself completely to my lips. I lay awake dreaming of the time when Janet would come to me and beg release from the torment of emotion that was growing within her and I would take her in my arms and teach her of the tender agony and small death.

I looked around the familiar bedroom. Some day this room that had been a prison of frustration would become a temple of love. The sunlight showing around the edges of the window blind would welcome us each morning to a world washed beautiful by our love.

Sunlight? I snapped out of my reverie. Our bedroom window never got the light of the sun until the sun was already high in the sky. We hadn't thought to set the alarm last night. What time was it?

The clock was facing the other twin bed, the one where Janet usually slept. I reached out and turned it around. It was eight o'clock!

I shook Janet's shoulder to awaken her.

"Five minutes more," she mumbled, burying herself deeper into the pillow.

"It's eight o'clock, Jan! We're going to be late."

She was awake and out of bed in a flash. I followed, going into the kitchen to start the coffee while Jan used the john. We woudn't have time for breakfast but both of us had to have a cup of coffee in the morning or we would go through the day in a semi-coma.

We drank the coffee standing up while we were dressing. Then we headed for the door. I had my hand on the knob when Janet reached up and kissed me quickly on the cheek.

I released the door and started to embrace her.

"We're late," she said and pulled away.

We ran all the way to school, too breathless to talk. We dashed into the building just as the bell sounded signalling the start of classes.

There was no opportunity to talk at lunch. Two other teachers shared our table in the cafeteria. We couldn't speak freely with them there and besides there wasn't any opportunity. Both teachers had recently had gastro-intestinal difficulties which they described to us in minute detail. For some strange reason I wasn't able to eat very much. My two gassy friends didn't have any trouble. They shoveled the food in like it was going out of style, meanwhile describing symptoms that would sicken a ghoul.

Janet was busy after school. She was having another appointment with the mother of the little boy with the overactive bladder. It was her night to do the dishes and I was supposed to cook dinner. However, Janet insisted that I was the only cook she had ever met who could make a steak taste like blotting paper. She said that she'd rather do the cooking herself that night than let me get near the meat. I gave in and agreed to do the marketing in exchange.

I got home from the grocer's a few minutes after Janet. She sat at the kitchen table telling me about her conference with her pupil's parent while I put the groceries away. We both worked ourselves up into a froth of indignation about it. Jan said that she had spent an hour trying to convince the woman that spanking her child wouldn't help him but she got nowhere. The mother still insisted that the best way to handle the problem was to apply the flat of her hand to the damp bottom of her son's trousers.

We reversed positions while Jan cooked dinner. The steak was ready and we were sitting down to eat it when it occurred to me that maybe we were discussing school matters so much because both of us were carefully avoiding another topic. We were both being obnoxiously objective because the closeness and intimacy of the previous night was not a thing which could be put in words. It couldn't be discussed and it couldn't be ignored. It could only be postponed.

We decided to put off having coffee until after I had finished washing the dishes. Then we could have it together in the living room. It was more relaxing that way. We often did that on Friday nights when we didn't feel pressured to get lesson plans for the next day ready. Then we'd sit in the living room drinking coffee and discussing the past week. We were still new enough to teaching so that we delighted in discussing the theoretical and practical aspects with each other.

On the Friday nights when we had dates with Bud and Frank, Janet and I would make extra coffee for the two men. When they came to pick us up we would all sit in the living room and drink the coffee for a little while before going out.

This Friday night we had planned to stay home and get our work done so that we would have the rest of the week-end free.

Janet said she was tired and would take a short nap. While I cleaned up. I was to call her when I was through. We would have our coffee then and get right to work.

Jan started to leave the kitchen then came back and stood close to me. "Darling," she breathed softly.

Here it comes, I thought.

She put her arms around my shoulders and repeated, "Darling, ... don't forget to scour the broiling pan."

I couldn't help laughing. Janet cut my laugh short with a quick kiss. She dashed out of the room before I could say or do anything. I remained standing in the middle of the kitchen stupified. What the hell was all that about? It had been a quick brush with her lips such as any girl would give another. There hadn't been anything to it except teasing affection. Nothing unusual about it except one thing—Janet had kissed me on the lips.

I gave up figuring out the subtleties of interpretation in absorption in the task at hand. Bet I'm the only human being in the world who has to concentrate when washing dishes. Think I'm kidding? I'm such a gook about housework that if I didn't concentrate completely I'd end up drowning myself in the dishwater.

As it was, I nearly wore my fingers off to the elbow trying to clean the broiling pan before I remembered that this was the twentieth century! The age of enlightenment! The acme of the industrial revolution! The emancipation of the housewife had taken place! No longer did women have to slave in the kitchen all day! Women had been freed by modern conveniences—like Brillo! I got out the box of scouring pads with the feeling of triumph of a scientist discovering a new catalyst.

The dishes were finally washed. I decided against drying them. Somewhere I think I had read or heard that letting them dry in the air was healthier. I think I heard that. Oh well, whether I had or not it would work as a good excuse for getting out of more work.

I started the coffee and took fresh cigarettes out of the carton we kept in the cupboard and brought them into the living room. No use having to make an extra trip if we ran out of them later. The coffee was ready so I poured it into the cups and placed them on the living room coffee table before waking Janet.

A last check and I decided that everything was okay and I could stop making like a housewife. I sat down on the couch and called to Janet to wake up. There was no answer.

I got up and went into the bedroom. Jan was lying curled up in bed with the pillow held tight in her arms.

I bent over her and tried to wake her by shaking her shoulder. Jan stirred slightly and turned onto her back. She opened her eyes and stared at me.

"Come on, Jan, the coffee will be ice-cold if you don't hurry."

Janet lay without moving, her eyes transfixed on my face.

"Jan, come on. Jan, an, oh-h-h. ... "

Janet had reached out her arms toward me in invitation I moved closer and bent down to touch the young body there on the bed before me.

Suddenly I was on the bed myself and I was holding Janet to me and Janet's mouth was on my face, on my mouth, following the line of my open-throated blouse. I could hear myself sobbing as from a great distance. Over and over I heard a voice that sounded like my own saying, "Janet, oh Jan, darling."

Janet got up abruptly. She stood beside the bed and reached down to unfasten my blouse.

I was wild with desire and fear. Was Janet playing a game with me? Did she want to see if she could arouse me? Was she going to drive me frantic with desire then leave me unsatisfied?

All my blouse buttons were undone now. I clenched my hand over Janet's to stop her.

"No. Jan, do you know what you're doing?"

"Just let me do what I want, darling," she crooned. "I love you and I'm going to show you how I love you. Turn over, sweet, I can't reach your skirt zipper."

And then I was lying on the bed without any clothes on at all. I knew that I should have been embarrassed, I had always been so modest in the past. I had always undressed in the bathroom and only come into Janet's presence when I had my pajamas on. But now there was a delicious aching happiness in every nerve of my body.

As I lay on the bed not moving, watching Janet taking off her own clothes, I could feel ripples of pleasure all over my body. As if I were being touched caressingly by Janet's admiring eyes.

Looking at Janet was like nothing I had ever experienced before. I had seen naked women: Karen and all the girls at school and at camp were extremely casual about undressing in front of each other. Yet, never before, I thought, had I really seen what a woman's body looked like. The beauty of the line from the high crest of the pelvic bone to the soft shadow of the inner thigh, the bright polished look of Janet's breasts swelling out towards me in the dim light from the living room.

Janet's body was beautiful before me and yet I felt an urge to touch it as it would become more beautiful when sensed through my fingers. Not realizing what I was doing, thinking only of the loveliness of the naked woman standing beside me, I began to move my body across the bed toward Janet.

Janet, her eyes grown bright and wide, breathed, "That's right, darling. Show me how you want me. Show me with your body."

My breath was coming quick and hard now. My legs, poised on the rim of the bed, parted and, lifting myself up slightly, I met Janet's lips with my own.

Fleetingly, I thought, "It isn't necessary, darling." But actually I was glad that Janet was telling me that it was all right, that she loved me and that she wanted to show her love in this way.

Janet accompanied her words with a rhythmic movement which alternately caressed and punished my body with her own. It was both a pain and a pleasure like none I had ever known before.

My body and heart opened out under these new sensations and spread to their furthest limits and then I was flowing out with my body to unexpected extremes. And in one moment of exquisite hurt my body was mine and then it was Janet's.

CHAPTER EIGHT

The next weeks were the happiest in my life. No longer did I have to hide my love for Janet as if it were something I was ashamed of. We gave our bodies to each other in the fullness and beauty of our love.

The only thing missing that would have made my happiness complete was the belief that it would last. The nagging fear that I would once again be raised to the heights of ecstacy and then cast down again to hunt among the shattered pieces of my heart for reason to go on living haunted me. Perhaps that's the reason I was overly-sensitive to any signs that Janet might be moving away from me. Maybe I was too anxious and, driven frantic with worry, I was responsible for the gradual wearing away of the fragile tissue of my own happiness.

It started only two weeks after the night when Janet had first given herself to me. Janet and I were alone in the Teachers' Lounge when Janet told me that she wouldn't be coming home for dinner that night. She had a date with Bud. We had been avoiding Bud and Frank for two weeks and I wanted to keep it that way.

"What do you want so see him for?" I asked, jealousy making me furious. "Have you missed not having Bud paw your body?"

"That wasn't necessary, Paula. I'm going out with Bud tonight because I enjoy his company. I know he wants to make love to me but he'll have to wait until I want him to. And so far I haven't wanted it. I won't want it ever unless our relationship becomes deeper and more meaningful than it has been. The feeling I'm talking about takes a long time to grow."

"You've known Bud almost as long as you've known me." My mouth was tight and my eyes were smouldering with anger as I came close to Janet and said softly, "It didn't take you so long with me."

Janet recoiled as if she had been slapped. "That…that's different," she stammered.

It was the first time we had discussed our intimacies outside of bed. I felt that the time had come for Janet to realize that there was going to be more to our relationship than just the pleasure of shared caresses.

Janet's protests had made me angrier than before. My words were like whips lashing her as I said, "Do you think that because I'm a woman our love-making has less significance that it would with a man? Let me tell you, it has more. A man and woman come together because of something basic to every human being. In theory, every man could make love to every woman. But in homosexuality there is no such instinctive drive toward each other. If you desire another woman it's because something about that particular woman is overwhelmingly attractive to you. Some people say that when women kiss they are making love to their own image of themselves. Maybe so. However, there is only one woman or possibly a very few in a lifetime who excites us with the realization that we want to blend ourselves with her. No woman, no matter how long she's been practicing lesbianism, could think of going to bed with the majority of attractive women she meets."

I stopped and stared unblinking at Janet. "Sit down, Jan. I think it's time we talked about this."

We sat down on opposite ends of the couch. I put two cigarettes between my lips and lit them. Janet accepted hers with trembling hand. We sat smoking in silence for several minutes.

I could tell that Janet's nervousness was growing in the silence. I suppose she couldn't figure out what I expected from her. A couple of times she opened her mouth to say something then shut it as if she couldn't think of the cogent observation I was waiting for.

I jabbed my cigarette out in the ashtray. "Look, Janet, let's understand one thing. We're both the same age so I don't want to hear anything from you about how I led you down the paths of iniquity. Okay, so I had had a love affair with a woman before. But you were the one who took the initiative in our relationship. I'll admit that I was awfully glad that you did. I wanted you to be my lover and probably I told you about myself because I knew it would bring you closer to me. I was in love with Karen but I've got a confession to make. I've been attracted to you for a long time.

"When we decided to live together I thought that nothing could make me happier than sharing the little details of daily life with you. This summer I realized that I wanted more from our relationship. It seems strange to say that my relationship with Karen made me love you more. What I mean is that through her I learned how beautiful a woman could be when she gave you her love . . . on all levels. Karen taught me not to be ashamed of my body. As I grew to experience my own worth I learned to appreciate other women."

I leaned back against the couch. "Say something," I demanded. I lit another cigarette and rested my weary head against the back of the couch, blowing smoke toward the ceiling

Janet got up and walked to the window. She looked out at the children playing in the schoolyard.

"I just d-don't know," she stammered. "Tell me more."

"Tell you? What can I tell you if you don't feel these things yourself?"

I looked at Janet standing by the window. She looked so young and defenceless. Those smooth tanned arms should be swinging a tennis racquet somewhere where the sky was blue forever and nothing more intense than a point match would cause the frowning concentration that now distorted Janet's face.

I began to feel as if I had been unfair. I was the same age as Janet but I had had a summer of growing while, in this context at least, Janet had remained arrested in time. Had I always had my present understanding? Hadn't I given Karen some rough moments—not through lack of love but because of the tactlessness of innocence?

"Baby," I said, "I'm sorry. I didn't mean to lecture you. Nothing is ever any good that's forced. You'll come to realize all the things I've been trying to tell you in time."

I stood up and took Janet's hands in my own. "Look, I've got an idea. When you see Bud tonight, why don't you invite him to come to our place a week from this Saturday? I'll ask Frank and the four of us can have a party."

Gratitude shone on Janet's face. "We don't have to have a party if you don't want one. It doesn't mean anything to me. I'd much rather spend evenings alone with you."

"Nonsense. You want to go cut with men. You'll get over that. For now, however, I won't force you to act like you don't. Besides, I like the idea of having a party. That way I'll be there to see that Bud doesn't try to horn in on my territory."

Janet smiled gratefully. "One thing, before we have the boys over, we better take care of having Helen Winsor to dinner. The other new teachers have all had her to their homes."

"Okay, you ask her. Let's make it sometime during the week so that she'll leave early."

We invited Helen to come to dinner Wednesday night. The party with the boys was arranged for a Saturday night two weeks later.

After dinner we all settled in the living room for a chummy chat. Real girly-girly stuff.

"Of course, I'd choose heaven for its climate but hell for its company." Helen Winsor's hearty laugh at her own humor was pitched low. The intimate sigh with which she seemed to indicate that underneath all this gaiety was a woman in noble torment was obviously directed toward the girl sitting at her feet.

Janet sat on the floor with her spine resting against Helen's chair. Her head, thrown back, was haloed by the lamplight shining on her long black hair. She was watching Helen Winsor with narrowed eyes in which admiration and deference were equally blended.

Overplaying the part of hostess, I kept running back and forth from the kitchen with clean ashtrays, pretzels, matches, etc. I saw the look in Janet's eyes and hated her for it. So that's what she was. A cheap fall-guy for a pseudo-sophisticated smalltown schoolmarm.

Helen smiled her favorite smile, the tragic one, as Janet fumbled with a book of matches, trying to light Helen's cigarette for her.

I jumped up from my chair and went back into my refuge, the kitchen. I turned the kitchen faucets on full force, drowning out the conversation in the next room.

Damn her, I thought. And to think that I had liked her when we met in New York. Of course, Karen had brought out the best in Helen. She was like a benevolent priestess when she was with Karen. In Karen's company Helen had been full of wise sayings and brimming over with a sympathy so warm I couldn't doubt its sincerity.

Brimming over ... Oh My Lord! ... the ice cubes! I shut the water off hurriedly and turned the ice tray over to find the cubes all melted. Well, too bad. That white-haired bitch had had enough to drink. And so had Janet. She wouldn't be making such an obvious spectacle of herself, mooning over that self-styled wit, if she wasn't liquored up.

Maybe she would. Maybe she doesn't care what she's doing to me? I slammed the refrigerator door shut with misplaced vehemence and stalked back into the living room.

"What do you think, Paula?" Helen asked.

"Think about what?" I asked, startled out of my angered reverie.

Helen laughed. "She hasn't been paying any attention, Janet. She prefers ashtrays to us." Her lower lip pouted out just enough to indicate that she knew she was being ridiculous and enjoyed the pose. "We were discussing your both taking classes nights at Wesleyan towards your Master's degrees."

"We couldn't do it. We don't have a car and Wesleyan's too far away. Besides, I've had enough of being a pupil. I want to sit on the other side of the desk for a while."

"Helen offered to drive us there herself, Paula, She teaches a class there twice a week and she says it won't be any trouble."

Oh my God, just like Shirley Temple! What was I supposed to say, "No, I don't want you to ride anywhere with that rapacious geriatrics case?" Janet seems to think I'm the only woman in the world who could desire her body.

"Come on, Paula," Janet said. "It would be fun if we all went together. Besides, we could use the extra money we'd make if we had an M.A."

Oh funzees! Would you like me to salt and pepper Janet before I hand her over to you, my dear Miss Winsor? Or do you prefer the unadulterated taste of young meat on your Jaded palate? Janet my love, you're a fool … or am I? Getting in with Helen Winsor would make things a lot easier for Jan around the school.

I realized that there was no gracious way in which I could indicate my displeasure at the prospect. "No. Count me out," I said. "You go, Janet. I'll stay home and stoke the fire and knit socks. I might even have cups of hot chocolate ready when you return from an exhausting session of Principles and Practices of Basket Weaving in the Elementary School."

"Yes, do start soon," Helen said to Janet. "I know you'll find it interesting and profitable and there are some very interesting people I'd like you to meet in Middlebury. People I know you'll like. Very understanding people."

Helen met my eyes in an expression of warfare. Triumph gleamed in Helen's eyes as Janet said, "Sounds great. I'm getting sick of eager young teachers."

After Helen left, we busied ourselves straightening up the apartment. We didn't speak to each other. There was nothing unusual in that. We spent many an evening secure in the knowledge of each other's presence, without words.

Janet smiled faintly to herself and hummed snatches of popular songs as she washed the dishes. Drying the dishes beside her, I knitted my brows and was silent. My damn jealousy was getting the better of me. Moment by moment the rage grew within me.

"I'll be loving you always. With a love that's true, always," Janet hummed.

The cup I was drying slipped from my hands and crashed on the floor.

Janet turned toward me and started to joke. "One more broken and we'll have to start using peanut butter jars. Paula, Paula, what's the matter?"

The towel was hanging limp in my shaking hands. My shoulders were hunched forward, hands stretched out before me, supplicatingly.

"I want you," I whispered in a hoarse voice that was strident with urgency.

"Are you crazy? Paula, we've got to finish these dishes and get our lesson plans set up for tomorrow. Can't you wait until we go to bed?"

"I want you now!"

"Paula, I don't like the way you're talking. I can't switch from washing dishes to love-making just like that." Janet moved closer to me and placed her hands on my shoulders. "Why don't you let a lady know you think she's irresistible in an apron? Might do something for her ego, not to mention her receptivity." She smiled coquettishly up at me.

My mouth twisted in an expression of scorn. "What you really mean is why didn't I warn you when I was going to interrupt your fantasies about Helen Winsor. It's much too rude a shock to abruptly have to think about going to bed with me when you've just been picturing yourself in her arms!"

"That's not true! You've been acting peculiar all evening and I didn't know what was the matter until now. I don't want anyone else. Only you, Paula. Do you understand me? No one else."

"All right, Godamnit, then prove it to me." I stepped forward and seized Janet's breasts in my fists and squeezed them. My lips found Janet's and fiercely I bit against them.

Janet twisted herself free. "What's gotten into you? Are you deliberately trying to bruise me?"

"Yes." My eyes were starting from my head, my breath coming in short gasps. "So that bitch can see tomorrow that you belong to me. That you're my property."

Janet stared at me, her mouth open in shocked disbelief. Then she lifted her hand slowly and smacked me hard full on the cheek.

Suddenly everything before my eyes turned red. In a red world I was energy incarnate. Dully, through my fury, I heard Janet screaming and begging me to stop.

Weariness at last came over me and with it the gradual realization that I was flailing about wildly with my fists and that in a heap at my feet was a disheveled young woman in a torn dress, her lips and nose bruised and bleeding.

"Janet, baby, what have I done to you? Baby, Baby, I'm so sorry." I knelt down beside her.

Janet looked at me dully and then a gleam shone through the haze of pain in her eyes. She reached up and hooked her arm around my neck. She pressed her mouth to mine and fresh blood oozed from her lips and flowed with her saliva into my opened mouth.

Tenderly Janet brushed my face with her fingertips. "See now I love you, darling. See," she crooned.

I was sobbing now and still Janet crooned softly as she reached up and dug her nails into my soft parts.

"Oh, how much I love you, sweet," Janet whispered as she ripped off my slacks.

Janet made love to me for the first time that night. Then she got up and went to sleep in the bedroom … leaving me naked and shattered on the kitchen floor.

Things went from bad to worse the night we had Frank and Bud over for the party. Everything was fine until we ran out of rum and pineapple juice.

Frank and Bud laughed unroariously as they mixed a fresh batch of punch. They extemporized an outlandish concoction from odds and ends they found around the kitchen. Cointreau and grenadine, a dash of bitters, a cup of cooking sherry, the contents of a small flask of pink gin Janet confessed to keeping in a bureau drawer for emergencies, and, at Frank's insistence, a sprinkling of nutmeg. Sampling the result, the men whooped delight at their own genius and demanded that we taste the liquid nightmare.

I portioned out the mess into coffee mugs and dropped whole cloves on top of each. This the men regarded as no less than an inspiration.

Clutching our mugs we moved back into the living room. Frank and I settled on the couch. Janet sought a straight-backed chair and, crossing her knees, placed her guitar on her lap. Bud sat at her feet looking up at her adoringly.

Janet ran through her repertoire from popular songs to old favorites. Soon we were singing folk songs. The sweet melancholy of *Greensleeves* and *Shenandoah* brought the group closer together in a mood of remembered regret—each of us for different things and different people yet we were bound together by the oneness of the human situation. Bud leaned his head back against Janet's knees and caressed her calves with his fingertips. He seemed to know the words to all the songs and the rest of us followed his pleasant tenor a moment behind when we were not sure of the next phrase.

Frank and I gathered up the mugs and went out to the kitchen to refill them. I welcomed the chance to be alone with him so that we could speak freely. Much had passed between us since that night in the pine grove. I felt it only fair to tell Frank about what had happened between Janet and me. He was genuinely pleased at my happiness. Frank and I were now buddies. Our one night of physical intimacy was a thing of the past to which neither of us ever referred.

"Bud's a great guy, don't you think so?" Frank asked.

"Yes. I didn't like him at first but he's been so sweet to Janet that I reconsidered. He's fun in a crowd too." I finished washing out the last mug and handed it to Frank to dry. "Frank, do you … is there anything between you and Bud?"

Frank laughed "No, of course not. We're just friends. Don't go projecting your tastes onto me. I've got enough troubles without liking boys. Me, I'm for women." Frank beat his fists against his chest and assumed an exaggeratedly virile pose.

"Lucky you. It's no joke being homosexual."

"Don't start making a martyr out of yourself, Paula," Frank said. "It's tough for men but you girls have it easy. You can live together, be seen everywhere together, and nobody thinks anything about it. Just let two men become more than casually friendly and someone is sure to start thinking things." Frank grinned. "And very often they'd be right."

"Ever tried it? With a man, I mean?"

"Ugh," Frank replied eloquently. "Have you? Ever tried it with a man? Besides me, that is." Frank blushed.

"Sure. I tried a couple of times. It was all right but it was never like it is now. Not like the way I feel about Janet. And, speaking of Janet," I took the dish towel from Frank and hung it up, "I wonder what they're doing out there? I haven't heard a sound from the living room for the past ten minutes."

Re-entering the living room we found that Janet and Bud had appropriated the couch. Bud broke away from Janet, his lips carmined with her lipstick.

"I guess we took your seat," Bud said.

"That's all right," I replied. "I have to go to bed now anyway. Got a busy day tomorrow."

"It is late. It must be…" Frank glanced at his wristwatch, "Lord, it's 2:30! Come on, Bud, let's let the girls get some sleep."

"Be with you in a minute." Bud embraced Janet again and sought her mouth, oblivious of the two onlookers.

Frank laced his arm through mine and pulled me with him out to the hallway.

"Janet's had a little too much to drink, Paula. They're just acting like a couple of kids, that's all. There's nothing for you to get mad about."

"Kid's hell! That little slut! Carrying on with him that way! And in my house!"

"Don't you realize that Janet's doing the best thing possible? She's protecting the reputation of both of you. You haven't been as careful as you should be, you know. For one thing, you look at her too much. Ordinary women don't do that. They look at another woman just long enough to estimate her worth as a competitor and then they direct their attention toward the men.

"And the way you look at her is all wrong too. At times you almost seem to devour Janet with your eyes. Every time you laugh you look into her eyes as if the joke were just between you two.

"You're together too much also. I've noticed the two of you meeting in the corridor between classes. And too often you sit by yourselves in the cafeteria. Paula, you better be careful or you're going to get in a lot of trouble."

"I don't care. I love her and it makes me feel dirty to think of sneaking around and hiding behind masks."

"Okay, if you insist on that attitude, face what it means." Frank smiled sardonically. "It means that you are responsible for what happens to that girl. As responsible as a husband is for his wife. If your actions make Janet lose her job, it will be up to you to support her.

"A man who loves a woman tries to protect her from hurt. You seem more interested in shouting your feelings to the world than in what the consequences will be for Janet. I don't know, maybe it has some cathartic value for you to be constantly acting out your emotions this way. But it seems to me that if you really cared about Janet it wouldn't be necessary to make such a hullabaloo about it. At times you seem more interested in the play than the characters involved."

"Oh, Frank, what am I going to do?"

"Right now you're going to put your arms around me and kiss me. I hear Janet and Bud coming this way."

"Come on, you two, break it up. Time to go home." Bud's voice was loud with the excitement of liquor and the nearness of Janet.

I tried my best to look properly sheepish as I pushed Frank away. "Goodnight, Bud, Frank, it's been fun."

"Boy, I'll say it has!" Bud laughed and pulled Janet to him. Liquor was making him unnaturally crude.

I winced and started to reply. Frank's fingers digging into my arm stopped me.

After the men had left, we undressed hurriedly and fell exhausted into bed. We never used both beds now. Every night we crowded together in one of the twin beds, welcoming the enforced closeness.

I was lying in bed, staring at the ceiling and thinking of how glad I was that Frank had talked some sense into me before I did something foolish when Janet interrupted my thoughts.

"Paula, would you do something for me?"

"Sure," I muttered sleepily, "what would you like?"

"I don't want you to ever go out with Frank Yellen again."

"What!" I snapped awake. "For Heaven's sake, why? I thought you liked him."

"I despise him. Would it mean so much to you ... not to see him again?"

"I'm not in love with him if that's what you're asking. I don't get it. This is a bit of a switch, you know. Why don't you want me to date him?"

"There are some things I just can't explain. If you loved me you wouldn't mind making a few sacrifices for my sake. It would please me very much if you'd do this one thing for me, Paula." Jan's voice was husky with suppressed emotion.

"It's late, honey. Couldn't we discuss this tomorrow?"

Janet reached over and put her arms around me, cradling me like a child.

"I couldn't sleep thinking that you don't love me enough to give up Frank for me. Don't hurt me this way, baby. It's not worth it."

"I didn't know my seeing Frank was hurting you."

"It is," Janet replied. "I didn't want to say anything but I had to let you know how I felt. Won't you do it ... for me?"

"I'd do anything for you, Jan. You know that."

The next day there was a letter from the landlord waiting for us. Several of our neighbors had complained to him about the noise of the previous evening. Janet handed the letter to me to read as if she accused Frank and me of having caused the disturbance while she and Bud were silently exchanging caresses.

CHAPTER NINE

had started it all. I had been responsible for the first orgy of jealousy. Just a little old trend-setter, that's what I am.

And like all good students should, the pupil came to surpass the teacher. Janet became suspicious of every woman I so much as said hello to. She refused to trust me out of her sight for a moment. I wanted to take graduate courses at Wesleyan like I wanted to chop off my big toe. Janet was determined to take the classes and insisted that I accompany her. I protested that I would just stay home alone reading on the nights she was in school. Janet said she couldn't trust me, I might invite someone over when she wasn't there. I said that if she had no faith in me she might as well forget about our relationship because I didn't want to spend the rest of my life arguing. Janet said that she really meant that she wanted me with her every moment of the day because she loved me so much. I said that she could stay home with me then. For once and all, I declared, know that I've made up my mind, I'm not going with you. Janet said I was. Guess what … I went.

Helen drove us back and forth. She also drove me out of my mind. She kept insisting on taking us to parties given by her "interesting" friends in Middlebury. I could have killed her for introducing Janet to them. Helen's friends were all very intelligent, very witty, charming and lascivious. They weren't all homosexuals. Most of them were just what you might call versatile. Too many of them for my peace of mind found Janet attractive. As far as I knew Janet never followed through on any of the contacts she made at those parties but she was very big in the come-on department. Man, could that girl flirt! She carried on with men, women, and every shading in-between.

I got a lot of attention too. We were new and young and Helen's friends welcomed us with open lids. I got a charge out of the fuss they made over me and it did great things for my ego to have three or four attractive women battle over who was going to sit next to me. They lanced attendance on me as if I were the most gorgeous woman on Earth and I loved it but they didn't really mean anything to me. I was so much in love with Janet that no one else stood a chance. I tried my best to convince Janet of this and got nowhere. She was constantly flying into a temper over my alleged flirting. If I had been merely civil to someone Janet would accuse me of having arranged a sexual assignation. When I managed to convince her of the absurdity of such a claim, Janet would switch to saying that the only reason I wasn't going to bed with someone else was that I was afraid she would find out about it. If I managed to shut Janet up long enough to protest that I didn't find the woman in question appealing, Janet insisted that I was unconsciously attracted to her and refused to acknowledge it consciously. How can you argue against something like that? Unconsciously I could be attracted to Margery Main and not know about it.

It was allright for Janet to bitch like a shrew about my behavior but if I said anything about the way she carried on I was made to pay for it days afterward. Janet insisted that she was never more than courteous to anyone at the parties and that I was distorting everything because I had a guilty conscience and was trying to prove that Janet was to blame for my perfidious desires. For days afterward she sulked indignantly and verbally. I soon gave up saying anything about Janet's behavior at the parties. It wasn't worth it.

When you feel about someone as I felt about Janet you are willing to put up with an awful lot. The short end of the stick is better than nothing at all. Once again I found myself under the power of a domineering woman who thought that fair play was whatever she could get away with. My eyes were wide open and I knew that Janet was using my love to make a slave out of me. I didn't care. Better a sexy despot than an untouchable friend. As long as I could hold Janet in my arms and hear her say that she loved me I could tolerate anything else she did. Once inside our little apartment she was wholly and completely mine and I was willing to ignore what happened at the parties so long as we ended up the evening alone at home together. Happy little masochist Paula Harman.

Driving back and forth to Wesleyan with Helen was a royal drag too. Something was going on in Helen's warped little mind that didn't make sense to me. She was playing up to Janet just as before. That much I had anticipated. What I didn't get was Helen's reason for including me in on her big pitch.

It wasn't just her way of paying attention to me so I wouldn't feel left out. There was more to it. Helen flirted with me as openly and as fervently as she did with Janet. I wasn't going to make an issue out of it by discussing it in front of Janet and since the three of us were always together there were no opportunities for a private conversation.

Aside from the unavoidable automobile rides, I was never alone with Helen because I deliberately avoided her like the plague. I didn't like dealing with her when we were in Oakwood because there she was Queen of the crap pile. As her professional inferior I would be at a disadvantage when discussing personal matters. A couple of times the three of us had dinner together even though I didn't want to. Janet insisted on it and my objections always stopped when Janet pulled the oldest trick in the books ... tears.

She cried a lot. Almost every time I tried to assert my nonexistent independence I was confused by Janet's sudden flood of sensitivity. She claimed that I hurt her feelings practically every time I wasn't tossing verbal bouquets her way. She knew how to keep me slavishly attentive. I couldn't stand to see her cry and all she had to do was get a little damp and I'd come through with a routine that made Valentino look like a slob.

Janet's fragile emotions were phony. I knew that. She wasn't as good an actress as she thought she was. The dam only broke when she wanted something from me. At other times I could have kicked her around the block and she wouldn't have pulled the paranoid bit.

Every argument was inevitably followed by a sleepless night of sexual excess. It was a good way to resolve things—up to a point. Trouble was there were too many nights when I was called on to prove my love over and over again until dawn. And there was little rest to be had most other nights when Janet claimed she was so much in love with me that it was agony for her not to lie in my arms and surrender her lips to mine.

Janet was no more of a nymphomaniac than I was. Her insatiable sexual appetite was designed to convince me of the intensity of her emotions. The lady protested too much.

Janet could arouse me beyond rationality with a smile yet always I remained aware of the painfully brutal deliberateness of her passion. There was nothing I could blame her for. Never in word or deed did she lessen her affectionate barrage. Every sacrifice demanded from me was matched by a voluntary denial by Janet. I had no tangible evidence of her insincerity until the night in April when Karen again visited Helen.

When Janet had made me promise to give up Frank I had taken it for granted that she would include Bud in the exclusion. That's only being fair. It was a logical conclusion. I didn't question it because Jan and I were always together, she never went out on dates.

Karen turned up without warning. She just came into my classroom and seated herself at an empty desk. Karen was casual, poised and unnerving. She enthroned herself behind the tiny desk and smiled at me brightly. She watched me teach as if I were putting on a floor-show.

It was a warm day for April. The children were itching to get out into the sun. Friday afternoons are always difficult for teachers. Everyone is anxious to start the week-end and the teacher has to fight to keep her pupils attentive. Being a charter member of the TGIF (Thank God It's Friday) Club, I usually watched the clock even more than my students.

This Friday had been worse than usual. The warm weather made me lazy and I had given the class an essay writing assignment so I wouldn't have to work too hard. When they completed their assignments I had them read them aloud. I gave a brief comment on each one. I wasn't exactly straining myself.

As a matter of fact, I wasn't even giving the recitations the attention I should have. Most of my attention was focused on more relaxing things.

Afternoon sunlight bathed the budding leaves of the trees outside the schoolroom and threw warm shadows onto the walls of the room. Soft flickerings of light played on the children's upturned faces, making them part of the richness outside. The air, heavy with the torpid somnolence of a warm Spring day, made me feel like I was resting on a wind-couch of infinite softness. I watched the shadow patterns of the leaves on the wall, only half-listening to the recitations.

The last pupil finished his recitation and sat down. I mumbled some nonsense about his essay which I had hardly heard. Then I glanced at the wall clock. It was 2:30 and school didn't let out until 3:30. That meant that I had to dream up some way to kill an hour. I was fumbling around in my mind for an inspiration, unpleasantly aware of the small sounds of impatience the class was making, when Karen came in.

Her I needed like I needed a hit in the head. Her patronizing, amuse me, smile flipped me. My mind went blank. I couldn't think of a damn thing. The kids had been diverted briefly by

Karen's appearance. Then they again looked to me for direction. I had to act fast or I would lose control of the class irrevocably.

Karen saved the day for me. She realized my predicament and thought of a great idea. At first I thought that she had become a candidate for a flip factory. Karen pantomined drinking, talking, thought, inspiration and laughter.

Dulcie Harrison caught on before I did. "Oh, she's going to tell us a story!" Dulcie exclaimed delightedly.

Of course. Karen had been signalling that we should tell the kids stories which we made up as we went along as she and I had at camp.

Karen came to the front of the room and the two of us took turns in telling the wildest version of *Romeo and Juliet* imaginable. We were each good for about five minutes of monologue before supressed laughter threatened to overcome us and the other one would pick up the thread of the story. We had a ball. The kids ate it up. They were on the edges of their seats. I wonder what they'll think when they get old enough to read Shakespeare themselves and find out that Romeo wasn't a Mississippi riverboat gambler who met Juliet at an American Legion convention?

Karen had to dash off immediately after the 3:30 bell. She and Helen were going to a cocktail party in Torrington. I accompanied them to the car. From their conversation I gathered that Karen's arrival had been as much of a surprise for Helen as it was for me. A new schedule at the hospital where she worked gave Karen Fridays off. She didn't have to report back until Saturday afternoon. So she woke up this particular Friday morning and thought that she would like to see Helen and me. The idea was father to the deed. Karen got in that flip-top Social Security case she calls an automobile and drove directly to Oakwood, completely confident of her welcome and absolutely assured that the local pedants would cancel all prior engagements for the pleasure of her company. She was right.

We stood by the car talking for a few moments before they drove off for the party. Janet had bus duty that week. She was standing about thirty yards away from us herding children into the two antique buses. I saw her glance over in our direction many times. I got a little malicious bang out of pretending not to notice her. I knew that she was panting with curiosity.

Miss Lerner and Company would be back in Oakwood by eight at the latest. Karen suggested that we all (Janet included) get together and make the local cafe society scene (otherwise known as the Palace Bar and Grill). Karen said that she would be looking forward to meeting the legendary Janet. Her eyes sparkled with teasing challenge.

Helen seconded the invitation in a lifeless voice. Her expression as she glared at Karen was one of sincere malice.

Janet and I were to meet them at Helen's apartment at eight. From there we would all set out together for Oakwood's den of iniquity.

All the way home I underwent an ambulatory third degree. I had already told Janet almost everything I knew about Karen. She wanted to know more. All the facts had to be reviewed and correlated. Jan wanted to know all about Karen's psychological make-up also. I answered her questions as best I could, basing my conclusions on incidents from the brief yet frantic history of our relationship.

Janet asked enough questions to write Karen's biography. I couldn't answer some of them. Janet wouldn't accept my excuse of ignorance. She posed hypothetical situations in which I had to imagine I was Karen and tell Janet how she would react.

The only comment Janet made aside from her questions was to say that Karen was better looking than she had expected her to be. In fact, Janet said, Karen was quite beautiful. Also, she was hesitant about committing herself for the evening. We had both planned to just relax at home that evening so I knew she was free.

All Jan would say however was that she'd make up her mind after dinner.

The interrogation continued until seven o'clock. Time was running out, we had to bathe and change our clothes and walk thirty minutes to Helen's place. I interrupted the Grand Inquisitor, she had to make up her mind now.

Janet said she wanted to stay home. I suspected that I had painted Karen in such an unpretty light that Jan wanted to avoid her. I voiced my suspicion and extolled Karen's charm and intelligence. Jan assured me that Karen sounded like an ever living doll and she was looking forward to meeting her some other time.

Janet couldn't join us that night because she didn't feel well. She had a bad headache and her joints ached. She thought she was coming down with a cold and was in no shape to go out.

For a girl who talked about her infirmities as if she were one step away from death's door, Janet had had plenty of energy when she was questioning me earlier. There was something phony about her whole attitude. The most suspicious aspect was her willingness to let me out of her sight. She hadn't let me go out alone in months. This time she was insisting that I go without her to spend the evening with a woman she knew I had once loved!

Arguing with Janet made me late. I had to rush through a quick shower and dress hurriedly. Jan sat on the edge of her bed while I was dressing, coughing appropriately. By the time I left she had coughed so much one would have thought the poor girl had developed a case of advanced tuberculosis since dinner.

The chill night air took my breath away. A strong breeze was blowing in from the river and sweeping the tattered remnants of the day's heat away. I half ran the distance because of my lateness and also to keep warm.

Helen and Karen were waiting for me when I arrived fifteen minutes late. They had already changed clothes for the evening and were having one for the road when I came in. Helen mixed a drink for me and we all sat around talking for about an hour before going out.

I explained Janet's absence to them. Karen's reaction infuriated me. She just raised one eyebrow and pursed her lips as if to she didn't believe Janet was sick and that she suspected I had arranged to cut down on the competition. I frowned disgustedly and looked away from her. Then I noticed the expression on Helen's face. That unnerved me completely. Helen was looking at me sorrowfully and compassionately. She veiled her eyes as soon as she noticed that I was looking at her. What the hell was she pitying me for?

We finished our drinks and left the apartment. It was decided that Karen would drive us to the Palace Bar and Grill in her convertible. Helen opened the car door, then stepped back and gestured me inside. That meant I was siting next to Karen and Helen was on the outside. My dear boss was getting awfully magnanimous in her old age.

Chill air leaked in from a hundred places where the convertible top was loose. The wind had risen and strong gusts of it rocked the little car and thrust icy fingers inside. I began to shiver with cold. I was wearing only a light jacket over my dress and now that I wasn't keeping warm by running it was inadequate. My apartment was only a few blocks out of our way so I asked Karen to stop there for a minute while I ran up and got a warmer coat.

Helen directed Karen through the deserted streets. Most people probably were staying in that night out of the cold and even the trees shivered their branches against the wind.

There was a parking space directly across the street. Karen nosed the car up to the curb and turned the ignition off. I glanced up at the windows of the apartment. Light was showing through the drawn blind. That meant that Janet was awake and I wouldn't be disturbing her.

Then two figures approached the window, dimly silhouetted against the drawn shade. They stood close to one another. A shadow arm reached out and embraced the shorter outline. They moved together and silhouetted mouths met.

A glance down the street confirmed my suspicions. Bud's car was parked near the corner.

"What ... ?" Karen started to ask.

"Get going and shut up," Helen said.

I was grateful for her understanding. I was speechless and numb. Helen covered for me by chattering away as if nothing had happened. She talked so much that Karen didn't have a chance to say anything. Thank God.

No wonder Janet hadn't objected to my going out without her. She must have been planning on seeing Bud and Karen's unexpected visit gave her an easy way to get rid of me for the night. Suppose Karen hadn't been around, what would Janet have done then? What had she done the other times?

I was sure this wasn't the first time she had lied to me. Oh no, too many pieces were fitting into place. Put them all together and the jigsaw puzzle spelled out the old one ... the lady protested too much. And I had fallen for the oldest line in the books. Jan had kept me on the defensive so much that I hadn't questioned her actions.

Compassion makes for strange bedfellows. Helen was coming through for me beautifully. All the time that I was recovering from the shock of seeing Jan in Bud's arms, Helen worked on keeping Helen off my neck.

I appreciated her efforts. For a change, I started taking Helen in without a smoke-screen of prejudices. I began to realize that she was really quite a fine woman. I was the one who had been unfair. Helen had never done anything to me. It was no crime that she had been attracted to someone I had also wanted.

Helen really shone in comparison with Karen. That became especially apparent after we had seated ourselves in a booth in the Palace Bar. Helen sat next to me and Karen was across the booth facing us. I was still too shook up to talk. The other two were joking around lightly and seeming to ignore me while I hit the Scotch like it was going out of style.

Karen was talking to Helen but she wasn't ignoring me. I could feel her leg moving rhythmically against mine under the table. She was wasting energy. I wasn't interested in anything like that at the moment. Also, I was a little bit offended by Karen's lack of sensitivity. She knew I was upset and yet she thought she could arouse me. Sex was Karen's answer to everything. She had the same faith in orgasms as an alcocholic has in a bottle of bourbon.

Helen's hand was resting on my other thigh. That was different. It was clear Helen wasn't trying to insinuate anything. She was trying to comfort me. It was a gesture of silent understanding and friendship. It was also the only thing that helped me keep control of myself and not break down crying.

At first I drank to relax and then I drank to get drunk. I succeeded in both. Thoroughly stinko, I put off thinking about my misery and joined in the general hilarity. We all had a fine time. I must not have been the only one who drank too much because I dimly recall laughing myself sick over Helen's description of the first time she went to bed with Sandra Munson.

We were kicked out of the place at one o'clock, the legal closing time. As soon as were outside and the cold fresh air hit me I became cold sober. That was bad, I dreaded going home and the inevitable confrontation with Janet.

Helen came through for me again. She told Karen to drive straight to her apartment and she would take me home in her own car from there. Karen made some obscene comments which we both ignored.

We were at Helen's apartment in what seemed to me to be a remarkably short time. Karen was really pouting by that time and Helen had to take her aside for a whispered conversation before she would go up to the apartment alone. Then Helen joined me in her car and we were driving slowly through the sleeping town.

We didn't speak until Helen had parked the car near my home. Then, she stared straight ahead at the darkened windshield for some moments before speaking.

Her words came, heavy with emphasis. "I wish to God you didn't have to go through this."

I waited, not speaking, for her to continue. She needed no encouragement.

"There's nothing I can do, though. You can only learn through experience. I could describe a peach to you completely and still you wouldn't know what it is until you had eaten one. I guess insincerity is another one of those things that must be tasted to be understood. Believe me, Paula, if I had thought that there was any way I could have prevented this, I would have done so. I knew it was hopeless. You wouldn't have believed me until tonight."

Her voice was so soft and gentle and sad that it broke through my reserve. Suddenly I was crying without shame.

Helen reached over and took my hand in hers. "We've never really talked before. I've been sorry about that," she continued. "I suppose it was inevitable under the circumstances. You had no reason to trust me then."

"I—I thought you were trying to take Janet away from me," I sobbed.

Helen smiled ruefully. "I thought you'd think that. You were wrong."

My tears were subsiding as a feeling of wariness crept in. "Helen, I saw the way you looked at Janet. You can't deny you were attracted to her."

"I'm not denying it. I was attracted to her and I still am. That isn't enough to make me to break you two up though. I'm just not that kind of person. If I were in love it would perhaps be different. I'm not in love with Janet. Please believe me, Paula. I'm being as honest with you as I can be.

"I could have loved Janet except for one thing. I'm too old to go through what you're going through tonight. You see, I knew this was going to happen. I knew because I sized Janet up for what she is long ago. Because I have known other women like her. Because, when I was as young as you, I too gave myself fully to a woman who was incapable of love."

"Karen?"

"No, not Karen. She came later. It's not anyone you know. Her name doesn't matter. The point is that, like you, I wanted love and companionship and a home. I made the wrong choice. And I learned the hard way that the kind of woman who could share my life with me was hard to find. The others, the Karens and the Janets, are for filling in time. I'm all too human, I need lovers and friends even though I know that they're far from my ideal. Karen is charming, good company and I like to go to bed with her. If I didn't need sex I'd probably never bother with her. But sex and love are not the same things."

"What makes you think that Janet is like Karen? She said she loved me. Just because she saw Bud behind my back one night, it doesn't mean she'll ever do it again."

"First of all," Helen began, "let me tell you that they all say that they love you. Words are cheap. Secondly, Janet has already been unfaithful to you many times. This is just the first time you caught her at it. I hate to be the one to have to tell you about this but it's better that you find out now."

I couldn't believe what Helen was trying to tell me. It was impossible that Janet had been living a lie. She was so loving, so much more wonderful than I had ever dreamed anyone could be. "You're lying! You have no proof!" I spat out.

"No, I'm not lying. I hope you're not going to hate me for this," Helen stopped and sighed deeply before going on. "I know Janet's been unfaithful to you. I know it because she's told me about it. Because she's tried to go to bed with me. No, Paula, I've never made love to Janet. That was my choice, not hers. Several times within the last three months she's been alone with me when you didn't know about it. Each of those times she tried to seduce me. I resisted her because I didn't want to hurt you or myself.

"Think back. Remember the night you had a virus infection and couldn't go to your classes at Weslyan? Janet and I didn't go to school that night either. We stayed in my apartment. And then there was the night when you had to get all your grades in and Janet finished hers long before you did. She went out for a long walk that night and left you alone to finish your work, remember? Well, that long walk took her to my place. I wasn't expecting her and had already gone to bed but she insisted on coming in. She would have stayed half the night if I hadn't thrown her out at midnight. She probably was back home by about twelve-thirty, right?"

I nodded a mute affirmative.

"I wasn't the only one receiving the attentions of our faithless friend. She's been seeing Bud right along. Two occasions which I know about are the week-ends she supposedly spent with her family. She actually was with Bud in New York. I can even tell you the name of the hotel they stayed at one of the times and their room number. I know because I was in New York that week-end and I had a drink with them in their room."

Silent tears had been coursing down my cheeks. Now, they reached flood proportions. Loud sobs tore from my anguished throat. I heard what Helen was saying yet her words had no meaning to me as specific things. My mind could seize on only one thought which every new proof of Janet's infidility only intensified. One word swirled around and around in the chaos inside my head ... loss. Loss of Janet, loss of love, of faith, of belief and, in a very real way, loss of youth. Never again would my heart swell with the openness of youth.

Helen gathered me to her. Her arms were tight around me as I sobbed against her shoulder.

"Oh, Helen, what am I going to do?" I finally managed to gasp.

"You're going to do just what I've been doing," she answered. "You're going to teach yourself to recognize when you've made a mistake and not try to throw good emotion after bad. Janet is what she is and you can't change her. It's not her fault that she's the way she is. Loving Janet was your life. Janet tried to match your intensity but it wasn't in her. She couldn't really take your affair seriously. She never will give everything to a relationship until she's married and has children. That's what Janet was made for and everything else along the way just serves to feed her need for dramatics, companionship and sex.

"You're not like that. You're like me. Your goal in life is marriage with a woman. And until you find a woman who feels as you do, you'll be incomplete."

"It's hopeless. They're all like Karen and Janet. I'll never find someone to love."

"No, that's not true. They do exist." Helen paused, then she spoke with a gentle melancholy. "I know because I had a love like that once. She was one of those rare women who have the depth and courage to give themselves completely. We were completely happy for three years."

"Why did it end then? Can't that kind of relationship last?"

"It can last, Paula. I believe that will all my heart. If I didn't, I don't think I could go on living. You see, I'm convinced that we would still be together if…" Helen's voice broke, "if she hadn't had too much courage.

"You remember about fifteen years ago when the Ringling Brothers Circus had that big fire in Hartford? She was there, with her niece and nephew. She managed to escape with her neice but the little boy became separated from them in the panic. Her only thought was his safety. She made sure her niece was safe then ran back inside the burning tent to get the boy. She never came out."

"Oh, God, Helen, I'm so sorry."

"You needn't be. I've had three years of wonderful loving happiness. Most people never have that. And my heart wasn't buried with her. I can still love, though perhaps not in quite the same way. Anyway, I'm sure that eventually I will meet another woman with whom I can share my life. If there was one like that there must be more."

CHAPTER TEN

It would have helped if Janet could have read my mind. She couldn't of course and everything I thought of putting in words would have complicated the issue. I knew too well my beloved's ability to twist everything I said to her advantage. She would have me on the defensive if I said anything.

Because I couldn't speak I was forced to wait silently for something to happen. In time a solution did come to me. Time exerted its usual effect of emotional deadening. Couple that with the evidence I accumulated in the next month and you've got the whole formula. It was a formula that released me from tormented uncertainty and brought me to the point where I could tell Janet what I knew and how I felt about it. I could talk then because I no longer cared how she would reply.

Helen's revelations took the veil from before my eyes. I looked, I saw and I encouraged. It was the old technique of giving someone enough rope to hang themselves. It was ridiculously easy. All I had to do was pretend to be ill on a night when we had classes at Wesleyan. Then I would call Helen's later in the evening. Helen made out I was one of the other teachers during our phone conversation. Frequently I would ask Helen to tell Janet some little piece of gossip which Janet would repeat to me when she got home. Proving incontrovertibly that she had been with Helen that evening.

One week-end I told Janet I was going home to visit my mother. She knew that was unlikely. She knew enough about my relationship with my parents to be sure I'd only see them when it was unavoidable. The fact that Janet didn't question me was suspicious in itself.

I left Oakwood Friday night and took the train to the next station where Helen met me and drove back. I stayed with her that night. The next evening I returned to my own apartment. I had a story prepared to tell Janet. I was going to say that my decision to return was a sudden one prompted by an overwhelming desire to be with her.

My unannounced appearance provoked such chaos that I never got a chance to use the story. I checked my watch just before inserting my key into the door lock. It was 9 P.M. Saturday. I opened the door and walked into the darkened living room. I turned on a lamp. Almost simultaneously there was a gasp and the sound of hurried movements coming from the bedroom. A line of light appeared under the edge of the closed bedroom door.

There was no need to push it. I just sat down on the living room couch. A few minutes later Janet came out. She was trying her damndest to appear nonchalant. She explained to me that she had been freshening her make-up when I came in. I didn't bother asking her if she always locked the bedroom door before applying lipstick. Also, I didn't comment on her incongruous clothing. It was odd, however, that she had taken the time to put on slacks and a blouse and had apparently forgotten to don a brassiere. Some girls could get away with it but Janet's full breast sagged and pulled lushly at the straining buttons of her blouse.

Not being Tarzan, Bud was trapped in the apartment. The only exit was the front door and that meant going past me in the living room. The bedroom window was sixty feet from the ground. The nearest tree was about ten feet away.

Janet explained that Bud had "unexpectedly dropped in" and that he was in the john at the moment. That much was true. He was in the bathroom putting his clothes back on.

Oddly enough it didn't hurt to find him there. I was convinced before I even opened the door that he would be. I accepted his presence as just another proof, the way I would accept the sum of an added up column of figures.

I played it straight too. We all went out to a roadside bar for a couple of drinks afterward. Janet and Bud were nervous at first but I acted so unconcerned that they relaxed after a while. We talked and laughed and drank as if nothing had happened.

Later, when we were home alone, Janet made fierce love to me. That hurt. I couldn't block from my mind the torture of knowing that she was seeking the release with me which she had not gotten from Bud. He had gotten her all hot and bothered and I had stopped them. Janet had waited in frustration for one of us to finish the job. It didn't matter to her which one of us it was.

The end of the day was the hardest part for me. From the early days of anguish to the later ones of indifference and remorse, Janet never ceased to be desirable to me. She was a beautiful woman who would be physically attractive to anyone. My body had become too accustomed to caresses for me to resist. It was different when I held Janet in my arms, though. Now there was a hollowness, an emptiness. I loved her body with my own and my heart and mind cried out against this hypocrisy.

Sometimes Janet's endearing words lashed me like flaming whips. She said lovely adoring things in her passion. I knew them to be false. I listened to her and thought of her saying the same words to Helen and to Bud and possibly to others I didn't even know.

Things finally came to a head late in May. School would be closing in a few weeks and our long summer vacation beginning. We had planned to buy a car and motor through New England that summer. Before buying the car we were going to find another apartment closer to the school. We would sign the lease for the new apartment and move our belongings into it before leaving for our vacation.

We hadn't been able to find anything and had almost decided to keep our old apartment when a small house a block away from the school became vacant. Janet heard about it and came rushing home to tell me. The rent was low and all the other considerations almost perfect. Janet had talked to the landlord and we could have the house if we signed the lease immediately. Jan was all for rushing over to his office and giving him a deposit.

The time had come for me to make a definite stand. I told Janet I wasn't going to live with her in September and, furthermore, I was taking my vacation alone.

Questions, naturally.

I explained. Patiently, without rancor, I spoke of Janet's unfaithfullness, of her lying, of the hypocrisy that had sullied what I had thought to be a pure and beautiful love.

Janet protested. I answered with facts. Dates and names and places were listed. She had no answer. There was no answer.

We went through the next weeks like strangers. We were polite, too polite. There was nothing real to talk about any longer and we covered up the need for verbal exchange by exaggerated courtesies.

At last, school was over. Janet was the first to leave Oakwood. She packed her bags and waited in the living room for her father to come. I sat reading in an armchair.

When Mr. Coxe came in I put down my book and chatted with him. I even helped them load the car with Janet's baggage. When the last hatbox was stowed away, Janet said she wanted to take a last look around to make sure she hadn't forgotten anything.

Mr. Coxe stayed in the car. We went back inside the apartment. No sooner had I closed the door behind me then Janet was in my arms. And we were both crying and kissing and hugging each other tightly. And we were saying that once we had loved and once we had been together in a lovely dream that had to end because it was a dream. Then we stopped crying and Janet had to go. Our lips locked in a last kiss that was sincere and true because it was a toast to the unchangeable past and promised nothing.

I watched from the window as Janet joined her father and the little car drove away. I was sad yet not unhappy. I felt as I sometimes have when looking at photographs of myself as a child. I haven't forgotten how miserable my childhood was but there is something melancholy about the finality of its ending.

Janet and I would meet again. We would teach at the same school. We would be friends. Anything else was impossible.

Helen and I would be friends too. There was room for me in her apartment and I had accepted her invitation to live together in the fall. We were close as only two people with a common goal who have both known the same sorrow can be. There is a love between us which is based on a firm foundation of understanding and acceptance.

I started to pack my bags. I was going to New York for the summer. Karen was letting me stay in her empty apartment while she was at camp.

I don't know if I expected that I would find someone in New York. It didn't matter. I was in no hurry. All I was sure of was that someday, somewhere, I would find the woman who would love me as I loved her. Helen wasn't the one, though we both regretted our inability to feel more for each other than warm friendship.

Not Helen, nor Karen, not Janet. Someone, I don't know her name or what she looks like or anything about her. Only that as I write this she, too, is waiting.